NOR ANY COUNTRY

ALSO BY GARTH ST OMER

"Syrop" in *Introduction Two: Stories by New Writers*
A Room on the Hill
Shades of Grey
J—, Black Bam and the Masqueraders

GARTH ST OMER

NOR ANY COUNTRY

INTRODUCTION JEREMY POYNTING

PEEPAL TREE

First published by Faber and Faber
in Great Britain in 1969
This new edition published in 2013 by
Peepal Tree Press Ltd
17 King's Avenue
Leeds LS6 1QS
England

ISBN13: 9781845232290

INTRODUCTION

JEREMY POYNTING

> "It's amazing how those things affect you later on," Colin said. "At the time it's not nearly so important."
>
> — *Nor Any Country*

In *Nor Any Country*, Garth St Omer tells one of the oldest stories in literature, a *nostos*, a homecoming, and one that has a very particular pertinence to the twentieth century Caribbean. In the opening scene, the returning Odysseus, Peter Breville, is seen with his naiad, Daphne, boating on a lake in the most English of scenes in a London municipal park. Odysseus, a little research confirms, has a special attachment to the Nymphs of the springs, to whom he has made "many a solemn sacrifice".[1] The fact that there is a Penelope, Phyllis, waiting patiently at home for the past eight years, readers of *The Lights on the Hill*[2] will already know. But in truth, St Omer's referencing of the classical is merely playful and goes no further, except that Breville's snobbish friend Clive refers to his separation from the mother of his child who, like the weaving Penelope, is "only a seamstress", and to the social and intellectual inadequacy of his current partner, Hyppolita ("she's all right in a way, you know. She can cook. And she doesn't complain" (p. 31)). Hyppolita was onetime wife of Theseus, later put aside by him, and a few pages later the connection is made when we are told how Breville, seeking escape from his unplanned emotional attachment to Daphne, had "already been trying to thread his way through the labyrinth of their togetherness back to an original uninvolvement" (p. 34). What is more pertinent is Clive's introduction of the theme of educated men feeling shamed by their less educated wives, as Breville is destined to be in St Omer's next novel, *J——, Black Bam and the Masqueraders* (1972). In *Nor Any Country*, that marital catastrophe lies in the future.

Return is also a key topoi in twentieth century Caribbean writing, most famously in Aimé Césaire's *Cahier d'un retour au pays natal* (1939), but also as a key element in novels such as Claude McKay's *Banana Bottom* (1933), Neville Dawes's *The Last Enchantment* (1958), George Lamming's *Of Age and Innocence* (1960), and nearer to St Omer's time, Orlando Patterson's *An Absence of Ruins* (1967).[3] Patterson's novel, indeed, shares some significant features with *Nor Any Country*. Both have a male protagonist returning to teach at the university in Jamaica who has been changed by a relationship with a white woman in England, and both come back to a wife they don't love. What all these novels reflect is the situation that until the expansion of higher education in the Caribbean in the mid 1960s, it was the norm for the small minority with access to scholarships or private, family funding to seek higher education in the metropolitan centres of the UK, the USA and Canada, or in Césaire's case, France. But whilst there may be some slight allusions to *Cahier d'un retour* (French was St Omer's degree-level subject) in the sequencing of Breville's return – the street, the house, the mother, and to the father "en hautes flammes de colère",[4] which fits what we see of Mr Breville, the deputy superintendent of prison guards – St Omer's treatment of the theme is characteristically oblique. We see Peter making a pilgrimage to his parents' natal village, but his arrival there is never described, and whilst in many of the novels referred to above, the returning native has a political mission, St Omer's hero is merely passing through, wondering what to do about his neglected wife.

Like St Omer's other novels, whilst *Nor Any Country* can be read on its own as coherent work with its own thematic centre, it is linked by shared characters and their back-stories to two of the other novels. The characters of Peter Breville and his wife Phyllis have already appeared as minor characters in *The Lights on the Hill* in *Shades of Grey*, where we see, from the outside, and very briefly, the painful consequences of the Brevilles' reunion perhaps a year after the present-time events in *Nor Any Country*. As already noted, in *J—, Black Bam and the Masqueraders*, St Omer explores that reunion at length and from within, and also gives voice to Paul Breville, whose story is on the fringes of *Nor Any Country*. Each novel may be read separately, with comprehension and pleasure, but the full richness of what could be termed St Omer's "St Lucia Quartet" comes from reading all of them, preferably in their published sequence, and engaging with their different angles of view, the way they complement each other to provide a composite and intensive portrait of a particular place and time, and the way they offer rewarding patterns of similarity and difference among the distinctive gallery of characters the novels assemble.

The initial critical response to *Nor Any Country* reveals a split between those who admired St Omer's mastery of literary form, and those whose approach was more political – and much less admiring. For the *Asia and Africa Review* it was "a sensitive study of society and people in a state of change, which confirms Mr St Omer's standing as a writer of true quality and insight...";[5] *The Guardian* wrote: "The dispossession theme, of a man adrift between two worlds, has been worked over endlessly by Caribbean writers, but none with more economy and feeling than Garth St. Omer";[6] and Andrew Salkey on the B.B.C. described it as "a haunting, powerful and unique work of fiction".[7] The two significant Caribbean-based reviews, by Gordon Rohlehr in *Voices* and Edward Baugh in *Bim*, come to quite opposite evaluative conclusions, but one can read in their responses a degree of shared uncertainty concerning just what *Nor Any Country* is about. For Rohlehr, the novel is "the slenderest of St Omer's stories. It is too thin, too simply a catalogue of impressions to be sustained by the controlled, nostalgic prose of reminiscence which St Omer writes so well."[8] Edward Baugh's review is lengthy and enthusiastic. He judges that *Nor Any Country* "carries [St Omer's] craft nearer to perfection and assists in the bodying-forth of his view of things",[9] but says a great deal more about the craft than what this view of things might be. Whilst he deals perceptively with St Omer's treatment of the power of the Catholic Church in St Lucia, with the pursuit of the "bitch-goddess Success", with the alienation that makes Peter Breville leave Britain and with the compassion that characterises St Omer's writing, his most perceptive attention is devoted to the beauties of St Omer's prose. Like Rohlehr, he feels that "the main impulse of the writing is towards a portrait of island society", and he expresses some disappointment that St Omer leaves behind the inward psychological probing of Breville's consciousness that he finds in the first two chapters that deal with his life in London.

What is curious about both these reviews is that they bypass the main driver of the plot – the elephant in the room – which is what Peter Breville is going to do about his wife. Perhaps St Omer invests too much trust in the reader to make the connection between what happens in the marital bed and Breville's rediscovery of his island, but a pattern of correspondence and influence between the one and the other and consequent shifts in Breville's point of view is there to be seen. Indeed, if there weren't subtly threaded connections between the social and the psychological throughout the novel, then Edward Baugh's disappointment with the loss of the inward would be justified, and Gordon Rohlehr's charge of "thinness" and a "catalogue of impressions" would have some truth. However, Rohlehr's criticism of St Omer's prose as nostalgic also suggests that in seeming to want *Nor Any Country* to be a different kind of novel, he doesn't see what kind of novel it is.[10] This is a work that is primarily concerned with the complexity of moral choice (in the sense that a novel such as Flaubert's *Madame Bovary* is concerned with moral choice), that offers a psychologically profound exploration of the male psyche, unmatched in Caribbean fiction to that point, and scarcely since, and a vividly breathing portrait of the motivations, needs, strengths, weaknesses, temptations and learnt experiences of his central character. In the portrayal there are frequent, but quietly signalled, gaps between Peter Breville's state of mind – in which nostalgia contributes subtly to the undermining of his better judgement – and St Omer's resolutely unsentimental view.

The fundamental issue facing Peter Breville when he returns for a week's brief visit home, before flying on to take up a lecturing post, is how he should behave towards his abandoned wife. It is evident that he has never loved her, has married her only because she refused to have an abortion, and not marrying her would have lost him his scholarship. He has always suspected that Phyllis Desmangues has engineered the situation to escape from her own desperate plight after the death of her white father, who leaves his black and brown family unprovided for, to secure her future by marriage to a boy with prospects. At the time of the marriage, Peter is around eighteen. There have been, before he left, only "brief insensitive couplings" (p. 33). He has not written to Phyllis whilst he has been away, for three years as an undergraduate in Jamaica, and five years completing a doctorate in London, even when he hears from his mother that the twins that Phyllis gave birth to have died, and that Phyllis herself has been seriously ill, but recovered. Peter, we are told, had put a "hood over his emotions" as an undergraduate, and had "closed his eyes behind the slits of that hood" (p. 62) when he first arrived in London.

However, during his years in Britain, Breville's involvement with two women has opened up his mind to what an emotionally engaging relationship could be. His brief affair with Anna, which ends when she discovers Phyllis's existence, introduces him to unrequited passion, and his relationship with Daphne, though it begins with having no strings of commitment, teaches him what a mutually caring and sexually fulfilling attachment can offer. He knows that in the years away, the intellectual and experiential gap between himself and Phyllis will have grown even wider. We already know what happens to the relationship in *The Lights on the Hill*, where Breville is witnessed fighting violently with Phyllis, engaging in a very public affair, and being seen regularly drunk. It seems evident that Breville's resumption of the marital bed and his decision to take Phyllis (and his nephew Michael) with him to Jamaica is not the choice he should have made. So why does Peter Breville make that choice? That is the core question of the novel, explored in the context of an acute, but often implicit, portrayal of a particular time and social space.

That particularity is worth noting, because the eight years that Peter Breville has been away from St Lucia have been economically and socially very significant ones, marking the beginnings of a shift from a decaying plantation-mercantile society for which the word "feudal", though historically inexact, conveys a degree of truth, to one that is being incorporated into the modern world of international capitalism.[11] In *Another Place, Another Time*, set in time just before Peter Breville's departure, we are told that Derek Charles's mother could not vote because she is too poor. It was a time when the legislative and executive councils still comprised colonial officials and mainly nominated members, when the authoritarian structure of the sugar estate still dominated the rural economy, and the brutal labour of coaling ships (such as Stephenson describes in *The Lights on the Hill*) was an important source of working class, mainly women's, urban employment. It was a time when the Catholic Church, led by white French priests, had an almost unchallenged grip on the social and moral order. By the time of Peter's return, there has been full adult suffrage for some years, an elected legislature, and a degree of self-government, though with very limited internal powers. As Keith Austin contemptuously complains, "carpenters and clerks [...] ran the country now" (p. 82). This, though, is nothing like as significant as the changes in the economy with the new internationalised industries of banana export and tourism taking over from sugar. Peter's friend Colin tells him about "the big hotel they've built near La Colombe [...] you won't recognise the place", whilst his mother complains that she can't get lobster because the "fishermen selling all to the hotels". Peter does get to eat lobster, at one of the hotels, where Colin tells him their food is "all imported from America [...] Even the man who cooked it" (p. 71). In the town, now full of consumer goods in the stores, Peter feels he "might have been walking in a hot, drab, imperfectly imitated miniature of a metropolitan shopping centre" (p. 119).

Land, too, has become a keenly traded commodity. As they drive through the countryside, Colin tells Peter, "All this land you looking at gone, you know [...] Foreigners. They've bought all the damn place" (p. 76), but evidently not all, since Colin adds, "I managed to get a few small pieces", and Peter knows from his smile that he doesn't mean small. When they visit the Austins, their land "stretches for miles", bought cheaply, in parallel with Keith Austin's political career as the first black islander to penetrate the white and brown establishment. Austin's land is laid down in bananas, which contrary to neo-liberal propaganda was an industry dominated by the big estates, and a monopoly exporter. At Colin's party, where Peter meets his old school acquaintance Sydney and asks him about the family business (which had been in retailing), Colin adds to Sydney's "Can't complain too much", with "Not when you're shipping bananas by the tons every week" (p. 90).

Even the Catholic church shows signs of change, having been forced by the incursion of protestant missionaries to start training a few black priests, who, if Fr Thomas, whom Peter meets on his visit to his parents' village, is representative, are less inclined to hold a narrowly sectarian, eurocentric and colonial view of their role.

Most pertinently for the novel, the period of Peter's absence has seen the emergence of a new middle class of men who have come back (a good few with white wives) after higher education abroad. As Peter discovers, "It was so easy to be accepted in the still small group of returned professionals and their wives on the small island" (p. 79). However, St Omer also reveals that these apparently easy relationships still depend largely on "the surface togetherness of the classroom" and that, reflecting the reality of persisting racial identities and white economic power, "It was still 'you boys' on both sides" (p. 94). At Colin's party we register the uneasiness when Sydney reminds the group of Peter's nickname, *Pine Boeuf*, a reference to the size of the black scholarship boy's penis, made in what was then, no doubt, still a mainly white and brown school. All of this, St Omer shows in passing, in the course of Peter Breville's journeyings across the country – made as much to avoid being stuck in his parents' small house in the town, as from any desire to reconnect with his landscape.

But the transformation of the society is far from complete, a reality economically conveyed in the image of Colin's big American car driving through "small villages consisting of huts on either side of the main road" (p. 76), or Fr Thomas's mother who, despite his relaxed informality, insists on calling her son Father. At home, Peter's father might bridge the old colonial state in his occupation as a prison warder and the new world of modernity with his car, but his mother, ruled by the chimes of the church bells ringing out the times for prayer, still belongs to the old St Lucian world, and Paul, disgraced by his refusal to marry his pregnant girlfriend, remains trapped by the social power of the old morality. But change there has been, and Peter's years away and his new status give him both close-up access to it and challenge him to locate himself in relation to it – and by extension to Phyllis, who has not been part of those changes, and remains in the old world of moral obligation.

Over the week of Peter's stay, his shifting relationship to this changing world is mapped step by subtle step with the changes in his relationship to Phyllis. We don't know what Peter intends before his arrival, though he tells himself, on his first evening home, that "marriage [...] was only a word" (p. 44), and dismisses it as a colonial imposition: "A gesture that, like so many others, they had imitated" (p. 45), but he is clear that "It was a stranger he returned to. And a reminder of his expediency". We see him offloading his regret over that expediency onto Phyllis, resenting "the assurance with which, over eight years, Phyllis had waited for him" (p. 57). How then does he move from the position where he merely fudges an insincere promise that he will send for her once he is settled in Jamaica, to actually taking her and Michael with him? John Thieme sees this change as the "product of a conversation with Paul" and that it "seems to indicate a new awareness of social responsibility on Peter's part",[12] but St Omer is far more of a scrupulous realist than to allow for such a simple change of heart. What he shows is a much more gradual and, on Peter's part, self-deceptive shift in perceptions, that looks back to his past experiences, examines his characteristic motivations and his responses to emotional crises, and tracks backwards and forwards from the narrow space of the marriage bed to the openness of the countryside he escapes to with Colin. As a good realist, St Omer also recognises the role of some crucial catalysts in the process: the power of nostalgia, the shortness of Peter's visit, the sexual presence of Phyllis's body and, not least, the effects of alcohol on his moral judgement.

At the beginning of the novel, Peter is ambivalent about his return. After his experience of racism, so economically conveyed in the whispered greeting of the woman in the supermarket ("I see the niggers are here again" (p. 36)), he feels relief at leaving London, despite his bad conscience over forsaking Daphne. Already on the voyage home, he feels "an absence of tension and of strain" (p. 36). Inevitably he feels "apprehension" about what awaits him at home, but the "smiles and gestures" of surprised recognition he receives when he alights from the plane, "pleased him", and in the taxi from the airport "everything he saw and heard gave him back his identity, restored perspective and dimension, fixed him in place as well as in time" (p. 38). Later, when he looks from the verandah of his parents' house at the hills, it "seemed they had never been so green nor so close" (p. 50). This is the rosy glow of nostalgia, though not less real for that. St Omer shows, however, a steadily decreasing glow as the days of Peter's visit pass. Even on his second day, when he visits the market, "He did not find again the excitement" of his drive into town, and on his second drive with Colin, he "kept the excitement of his rediscovery in perspective" (p. 74) – not least because he is thinking about his drunken, lustful coupling with Phyllis the previous night. Peter is shown to be half aware of the effects of this nostalgic glow on his feelings, but, fatally, only half aware. When St Omer writes of how Peter "[...] had yearned, living in the metropolis [...] for the oasis of relaxation and friendliness the island, from a distance and in a time that was of memory only, seemed to offer" (p. 78), he offers commentary rather than access to Peter's thoughts. He wants us to see, I think, that Peter's stay is too short for nostalgic glow of homecoming to wear off, which it does, but too late, on almost his last night on the island.

Initially, Peter's responses to his homecoming and to Phyllis move in contrary directions. He is touched by his mother's happiness to see him and by the little episodes, like the gift of a morsel of meat and the brush of his mother's fingers on his lips, that make it seem "absurdly" that the "present had rejoined the past" (p. 46). He is moved, too, by the unwonted tenderness of "the touch of his father's lips on his lowered cheek", since their respective successes "had made them friends" (p. 46). Phyllis is associated with the claustrophobia of the family living room with its photographs of their wedding and the twin babies before their death. When Phyllis comes in, "Husband and wife kissed. It was like kissing Daphne goodbye before she went to work". As Peter stays up drinking to evade her, St Omer tells us how thoughts of the "marriage rattled in his unsober mind like cans on a cat's tail" (p. 45). Everything about Phyllis's presence is an intense irritation, as when she follows him down the stairs and ignores all his hints that she should leave him alone. Yet even on this first night of sharing their marital bed (when he keeps his distance from her), there are little incidents that hint at how some of his characteristics will undermine his judgement. We have seen some evidence of sensitivity and conscience in his relationship with Daphne (his mood of "self-indictment" over his "assumed exploitation" of her), and in his responses to his mother, but we have also seen a self-admitted capacity for expediency, such as when he pretends to be asleep when he wakes to hear Daphne weeping just before his departure. We see, too, an underlying vanity in his tendency to allow himself to be flattered, a word used three times about him, and displayed, without comment, in his behaviour, on a number of other occasions. Peter is certainly not without a capacity for guilt (he has after all been brought up in a pious Catholic household) but we also see how he is able to put his feelings at a distance. When he is in Jamaica as an undergraduate and receives news of his twins' death and Phyllis's illness, "It had been like receiving messages from a hilltop in semaphore" (p. 53) and he returns no signal.

In his interactions with Phyllis, we see, at first, a struggle between his rational if unfair perceptions of what is going on and his predilection for being humoured:

> He resented her humility, her apparent readiness to assume blame. Already, like Daphne's worrying when his work went badly, her assumption of blame had brought her closer to him. (p. 58)

He can recognise clearly what separates them, but turns that awareness on its head:

> She had not travelled to another part of the world, had not followed any paths of specialized knowledge, knew no sun that was not hot; she had not discovered, in herself or in others, human deceit and cynicism, had never known the delights of intimate human togetherness. She had remained in her world, been formed only by it, had waited in it with a confidence he found at once insolent and accusing, with a patience he could not help being flattered by. (p. 59)

Flattery that shifts his perceptions can also be drawn from others. When Peter meets his friend Colin on the second day of his visit, there is a piece of conversation which appears ironic (because of what we know about Peter's feelings), but which in hindsight can be seen in a different light. Colin, who has known about Peter and Anna in London, remarks:

> "Phyllis looking well, man."
> "Yes."
> "You're a damn lucky fellow, you know, Peter."
> Peter smiled.
> "You've had the best of two worlds."
> Peter smiled.
> "You scamp," Colin grinned. "You're not even defending yourself." (p. 70)

We see how Peter's desire to be thought well of by his wealthier friend leads him to lie about how his relationship with Anna ended, but we may also suspect that the conversation's importance is that it begins to show him Phyllis in a different light. We know Peter has a self-admitted tendency to be glamoured by wealth, class and lightness of skin. When he thinks back to his youthful relationship with Phyllis and her mulatto fairness, he acknowledges how he could still "never be sure how much her complexion had added to the flattery of her continuing, despite her mother's warnings, to visit him" (p. 63). He admits to himself, too, that part at least of Anna's attraction was:

> [...] the glamour of her background, her degree in Law, her parents' wealth and social position, her acquired taste and elegance. He was not sure how much Anna had been cause of, or later reinforcement for, his attitude towards Phyllis. (p. 76)

It is a nicely ambivalent passage since it implies a degree of self-criticism, and an admission of unfairness to Phyllis (and also that the advantages of class trump those of skin), but in the light of his implicit re-evaluation of Phyllis after Colin's party, it would seem that part of him at least continues to think of her lightness as a social advantage. But this comes a little later. What advances his connection with her on the second night of his stay is of a decidedly more catalytic nature: the flattery when Phyllis buys him a bottle of the most expensive brand of whiskey ("He had been at once hurt and moved"); the fact that he has drunk "copiously, drowning his ambivalence" and is lying in bed beside an attractive woman. He persuades himself, in a curious choice of adjective, that it would be "melodramatic" not to touch her:

> [...] he had finally turned to that body which did not attract him, his lust aroused, and mounted it. The ease of coitus when he had not prepared her for it did not surprise him [...] he had lain upon her unloved, responsive flesh, her body moving beneath him and the pressure of her arms locked at the back of his shoulders

> testifying to the willingness with which she had received him.
>
> How long after that lustful coupling he remained awake, he did not remember. He lay on his back, prised away from contact with her not only by their perspiration and the heat their bodies had generated but also, his lust assuaged, by a sense of his own dishonesty. (p. 75)

The day after, in Colin's car, "he was still upset by his impetuous coupling with Phyllis, still flattered by her response" (p. 75). It is the flattery that outweighs his admission of dishonesty, and following the next day's visit to Keith and Gloria Austin (a distinguished and wealthy black St Lucian with his mulatto wife), on his return home he makes love again to Phyllis, this time, we are told, "deliberately, preparing her" (p. 88). They even talk afterwards, though he dozes off whilst she is speaking, but make love again the next morning.

The visit to the Austins is important because it not only shows again how readily Peter is glamoured by wealth, but because it indicates the space in his mind where Phyllis, whom he scarcely thinks about directly, might fit. St Omer draws a witty contrast between Peter's memory of being a bored listener to Bach with Anna at a concert in London, and his evident satisfaction in listening to Austin's scratchy phonograph records of the Brandenburg Concertos, drinking brandy and ginger with this very "Afro-Saxon" man. Yet this is not the whole extent of Peter's response, since whilst he is listening to the sound of recorders in the Bach, as well as evoking for him the image of the blond soloists in London, a mental image connects him to the black culture of the island, of costumed masqueraders and of a woman "blowing on a bamboo flute, not elegantly [...] but furiously, her black face intent under her colourful turban, her eyes closed [...]" (p. 85). These two images suggest the poles of cultural reference in Breville's mind, with neither of which he is entirely comfortable, though both in their different ways attract him. We may note his fascination and terror with the masquerade devil figure he fears is chasing him as a child (pp. 48-49). These images connect to his reflections during and after his visit to the Austins about the race/colour dimensions of male/female relationships, how Keith Austin might have wanted a white wife, but settles for a light brown woman with whom he has found evident contentment. In the context of these reflections, and the images of the white and black musicians, Phyllis is a glaring absence, but one can deduce, in both his conscious and subconscious mental operations, that Breville is creating a space within which she can be located to his satisfaction.

Certainly, the following day, when the Brevilles attend Colin's party, Peter acknowledges to himself that "Phyllis looked very well indeed". More importantly, she evidently does not embarrass him, spending most of the time "speaking in low tones" to Helen, Colin's English wife. The potential of embarrassment is clearly on his mind, though, since "More than once observing her", he recalls Clive's talk of wanting a woman "I won't be ashamed of. A woman I can take out, man..." (p. 92). Evidently, Phyllis passes this test, for on their fourth night together, "He and Phyllis made love again and Peter kissed her for the first time" (p. 97).

The next two days Peter spends out of the capital, travelling to his parents' village. All this is neatly plotted, because the visit to the country both removes Peter from further interaction with Phyllis and the chance of some incident that will reveal to him how delusional his view of their relationship is, and returns him to a state of rosy nostalgia for his island. By the time he comes back and is confronted by Paul, and in particular by Phyllis's declaration of a hoped-for pregnancy, it is too late to pull back.

The evidence that his feelings about Phyllis are based on an illusion is further suggested by the fact that whilst he is on the motor launch heading round the coast to the village, he doesn't appear to think about her at all, reflecting only on

Anna and Daphne, rehearsing the contrary attractions of these two women. With Daphne, despite what he regarded at first as her "unprepossessing" body, he recalls a tender response to her slowly-revealed disclosure of need, and his appreciation of her sexual generosity and flair, and of the mutuality of their companionship. With Anna, there has been the passionate pursuit of the unattainable: "No boyhood dream had contained himself neglecting his post-graduate studies [...] to be with a girl like Anna" (p. 101). There's his silent "squeal of triumph" in the brief but brilliantly detailed scene when he looks at his disembodied body reflected in the mirror behind Anna, an image which says so much about what is illusory in their relationship (see pp. 101-102). Though he never quite admits it – beyond reflecting that Anna is someone who would always "survive glitteringly" – most readers will have concluded that when Anna dumps him, it is also he who has had an escape from a capricious ("the intense weekend after months of absence"), egocentric woman, who would have played with him until she grew bored.

What we may guess, though, is that in rehearsing his memories of the two women who have engaged his emotional life, Breville is, by an act of displacement, thinking about Phyllis. The movement of thought is double-edged. If it suggests that he might be imagining Phyllis as a substitute for Daphne, the comparison also indicates a more destructive pattern: that there are likely to be substitute Annas in the future. This is indeed what has already been shown in *The Lights on the Hill* where, on the fringes of the main narrative, Breville is seen engaged in an affair with Jeannine, a fellow lecturer at the university.

The other important element in Peter's visit to his parents' village (besides the economic way it locates his alienation from the islanders, where his changed accent and inability to speak patois mark him out as a stranger), lies in what the conversations with Fr Thomas reveal. The young black priest, also a returned native, articulates a commitment to place and people that Peter has not really thought about, and only half understands. Fr Thomas, for instance, tells Peter that his priestly separation from his parents feels as much an abandonment as a fulfilment of their ambitions for him, that "a priest is not something my parents can afford. I feel like a luxury, an extravagance. Do you understand that?" (p. 115). Peter clearly does not, and without needing to expand the contrast, St Omer makes it clear that whilst Fr Thomas struggles conscientiously to deal with the contradictions of managing his relationship to his people, from whom his role and education separate him, Peter, like Derek Charles in *Shades of Grey*, "had no cause nor any country now other than himself".[13] Peter is also silent and disbelieving when Fr Thomas paints a picture of Peter's potential as a transitional man, a bridge between his parents and his children, past tradition and future modernity, that he, by virtue of his celibacy, can never be. Fr Thomas tells Peter, "You will join what you have known to that which you will never know" (p. 116), assuming wrongly, because of the journey Peter is making, that he shares his commitment to making that connection.

The exchanges with Fr Thomas are important because they remind us that the moral choice Peter has to make in his personal life has a wider context in his past and present social and political attitudes. Peter, it will be recalled, was once the boy who remained loyal to his proletarian friends from the wharf despite the beatings he receives from his father (p. 43, p. 60). He recalls, too, a conversation he has had with Colin and Helen in their bedsitter in London, when he reflects privately that "a process of copying and imitation, begun on the island's sugar plantations, continued still" (p. 95), and how in their mimicry, the new middle class are the "new interpreters, direct descendants of that first expediently opportunistic slave" and concludes that "no one knew how long they would continue to be the clowning interpreters most of them were" (p. 96). Again, despite his attraction to the lives of the wealthy, Peter is shown not to have lost his sense of his origins, and how that still shapes his place in the world. After his meeting with Sydney he reflects that the new ease amongst the middle class, between the old white elite and others, is illusory:

> [...] the groups were still separate. They were like opposing teams running, from the starting point of owners and owned, in lanes on a track where the curve was only an optical illusion and the staggering was an advantage to some and a disadvantage to the others. Even now the distance between them, between Colin and himself on the one hand and Sydney on the other, still remained. (p. 94)

Peter, then, is shown as a man who vacillates between contrary attractions, between what he knows as a political and historical reality, and between his temptations to personal advantage and expediency. The outcome is his sense of solitary isolation, revealed in his reverie about the Colonial Governor, whom he imagines on a beach he passes, "lamenting his loneliness" [...] forced [...]to keep himself aloof [...] from his compatriots", a "dutiful and principled man", who is dedicated to preserving justice, but only "within the sphere of a greater injustice he had nowhere in his diary questioned" (p. 77). The reverie concludes, "It was not thus he liked to look at the dead man" (p. 78). In his review, Edward Baugh comments on the beauty of the passage, comparing it to Walcott's "Ruins of a Great House", but its fictive significance is as a projection of Peter Breville's state of mind. He too is in a state of isolation, suspended between his family and the middle class he can imagine himself joining, and also having to look at himself as a man challenged to be "dutiful and principled".

We never know at what point Peter decides to take Phyllis and Michael with him. The exchanges (see pp. 72-73, pp. 87-88) he has with his young nephew, where it is possible to observe him warming to the boy's vulnerability and eagerness to please, after his initial snobbish irritation with his patois-inflected language (p. 72) must be supposed to play a part. But it is clearly his exchange with his brother Paul that puts him on the spot about what he is going to do.

That exchange comes after his mother has at last tearfully confessed that Paul suffers episodes of mental disintegration; that the once brilliant schoolboy scholar and sportsman, who had the courage/arrogance to take on his society by refusing, unlike Peter, to marry his pregnant girlfriend, has been condemned to a humble warehouse job – often a sinecure because of his mental state – thanks to the charity of their mutual schoolfriend, Sydney.

What Paul's defence of his strategy, of what he claims is his feigned madness, reveals to Peter is what might have been his fate had he refused to marry Phyllis. It is the fate that Stephenson fears after his disgrace in *The Lights on the Hill* of "a long steady descent into rowdyism, squalor and every other kind of degradation."[13] It connects to the fate of isolation and despair that John Lestrade in *A Room on the Hill* never quite totally succumbs to, when Paul tells Peter, "It was better to be nothing than to be what I knew I could only become thinking always of what I might have been. I became nothing. I am nothing" (p. 122). Peter's concern in all this is Michael's position, and we may suppose that what is at work in his mind are the inversions of consequence in his and his brother's lives. He has married, his children are dead, his wife is alive. Paul refused to marry, his girlfriend is dead by suicide, his child is alive. That, reinforced by Paul's countering of what he takes to be Peter's accusation of selfishness in his treatment of Michael: "You think you're too good for her, too educated. You've left her alone here for eight years!" (p. 122) is surely enough to drive someone who wishes to be thought of as a decent man – and perhaps to be one – to ask Paul if he can take Michael with him.

In what is a brilliantly, but seemingly casually plotted novel, the final scene takes place, appropriately, in Peter's and Phyllis's bed, a denouement that is as chilling as Graham Greene's conclusion to *Brighton Rock* (1938), where Rose has yet to discover the message of hate that Pinky has recorded for her. In *Nor Any Country*, there is no actual recorded message of hate (but perhaps *Brighton Rock* is referenced in the "record one had made long ago"?), but Peter's train of thought – after Phyllis has told him, to his intense embarrassment, "Peter, I love you. I love you, Peter", and that she may "even be pregnant" – is a dark warning of the poison festering in his memory. This is the suspicion aroused long ago, when the evidence of her existence makes Anna leave him, to "construe Phyllis's tearful decision not to abort as plan [...] cunning and deceit" (p. 62):

> And the fear, Peter thought, the fear, and the memory, and the suspicion. It frightened him exceedingly that she might be pregnant. As if this pregnancy, as yet only possibility, travelled hummingly along lines to join the fear and the panic of the first. It was like listening, in the dark, to a record one had made long ago. The sounds he listened to evoked gestures and postures he did not wish to remember. Lying on his back on the bed, he felt suddenly weary. (p. 124)

Of course, the story that St Omer does not tell is that of Phyllis, but in his next novel, *J—, Black Bam and the Masqueraders*, she enters the action in a very physical way.

The subtlety of St Omer's treatment of the connections between Peter Breville's psycho-biography and his engagement with the society, landscape and people he returns to has been noted. What has perhaps not been sufficiently stressed is just how absorbing and moving a human drama *Nor Any Country* is. Here is nemesis, concealment, revelation, love, intense rivalry, and the ironies of deception and self-deception in an intimate family portrait. And, as attentive readers of St Omer will discover, they are placed in the emotionally engaging position of being witnesses and overhearers, nudged gently now and again, but mostly trusted to come to their own conclusions.

Endnotes

1. Homer, *The Odyssey*, trans. E.V. Rieu (Harmonsworth: Penguin Books, 1946, 1975), Bk. 13: 355.
2. *The Lights on the Hill* is the first novel of the two that comprise *Shades of Grey* (London: Faber & Faber, 1968; and Leeds: Peepal Tree Press, 2013). *Another Place, Another Time* is the second.
3. Later novels and stories of return include Austin C. Clarke's *The Prime Minister* (1977), Caryl Phillips *A State of Independence* (1986), and stories in N.D. Williams, *The Crying of Rainbirds* (1991), and in June Henfrey, *Coming Home and Other Stories* (1994).
4. Aime Cesaire, *Cahier d'un retour au pays natal* (Paris: Presence Africaine, 1968), p. 32.
5. *Asian and African Review*, 9 May 1969.
6. *The Guardian*, 8 May 1969.
7. B.B.C. May 1969 (Faber notes on review comments).
8. Gordon Rohlehr, "Small Island Blues: The Novels of Garth St Omer", *Voices*, vol. 2 no. 1 (1969), reprinted in *St Lucian Literature and the Arts: An Anthology of Reviews*, Ed. John Robert Lee and Kendel Hippolyte (Castries: Cultural Development Foundation, 2006), p. 18
9. Edward Baugh, "Book Reviews: Nor Any Country", *Bim*, vol. 13 no. 50 (Jan.–June 1970), 128-130.
10. Gordon Rohlehr compares *Nor Any Country* regretfully to an earlier generation of fiction whose heroes return to "claim their place" in their societies.
11. See Tennyson S.D. Joseph, *Decolonization in St Lucia: Politics and Global Neoliberalism 1945-2010* (Jackson: University of Mississippi Press, 2011), pp. 21-50.
12. See John Thieme, "Double Identity in the Novels of Garth St Omer", *Ariel*, 8 (July 1977), 81-97.
13. *Shades of Grey* (Leeds: Peepal Tree Press, 2013) p. 190.
14. *Shades of Grey*, p. 101.

“He had no cause nor any country now other than himself.”

Another Place, Another Time

1

For hours he and Daphne had been rowing in the scarcely warm sun. Ducklings followed their parents in single files over the surface of the water. And a couple of geese, to the accompaniment of warning honks, sailed past, close to the bank, their young in a line between them. In his well-kept suits, Clive could have rowed here, for hours too, unharried, made hot or ruffled by no tropical sun.

"These girls are much more helpful," Peter heard Clive say again. "They're not like our girls at home. If you want something they help you to get it. They give, they don't take."

He and Clive were walking the cold wet metropolitan streets, their hands in their coat pockets. Under the short curly hair Clive's head, thrust forward, bobbed up and down as he walked. Lean and unwrinkled he looked twenty-five, not nearly forty-five years old.

"It's not that I'm a snob," Clive said. "It's a matter of intellect."

He poked the cold air in front of him with a gloved hand holding an unlit pipe. Once Peter had accompanied him to a tobacconist's. Clive who had no special brand, asked the seller to help him to choose one. Smilingly she suggested a cheap brand. Clive bought the most expensive.

"I don't want any cheap stuff," he told her.

And when they were in the street again, the pipe lit now in the hand that poked the air, he said, "You mustn't let those people get away with anything you know."

They walked on. The February drizzle was cold on their faces.

"You understand what I was about to say about our girls?"

Peter smiled.

"You mustn't think I'm snobbish."

They entered a pub. Clive brought out pictures of his child.

"How old is she?"

"Sheila's nearly eighteen. She's leaving school this year. She wants me to send for her. She says she doesn't want to stay with her mother any more."

Peter was looking at the photograph.

"You know her? The mother I mean."

"I don't think so."

"You must know the woman, man. A brown skin woman from ——. She's a seamstress. I'm sure you know her."

Peter handed back the picture.

"You think I should send for her?"

"I don't know."

"Hyppolita doesn't mind. We talked about it."

"If she doesn't mind..."

"Sheila's mother can't take care of her properly. She's only a seamstress. I must send for her. Eh?"

"I suppose so."

"She'll have more opportunity here. She has 'O' levels. You know?"

Clive sipped his beer, put the picture in his wallet and replaced the wallet in the inside pocket of his jacket.

"I used to like that woman. I mean Sheila's mother. But she was lazy. She didn't move with me. She wouldn't better herself. You understand? I left her behind. We were no longer compatible."

He had worked his way up, had never been to Secondary school. He had taken correspondence courses in Aruba where he had gone to work with the oil refineries. He had done a course in political science at a university after he was already thirty. He had just finished taking an M.A. He was working now with the —— Office.

"It's like me and Hyppolita."

She was the girl Clive had sent for six months after he had been in the metropolis. She was from one of the island's smaller towns, was what Clive would have called a "brown skin woman". For a while she and Clive had lived together in the island's capital where Clive worked with the Civil Service.

"I can't go anywhere here with *her*. You know that."

She spoke little English, but she was friendly and laughed a great deal.

"I can't even talk to her. I want a wife who's a companion, too. You understand? Somebody to converse with. Hyppolita doesn't understand me when I talk. She's all right in a way, you know. She can cook. And she doesn't complain. For two years while I was studying at night she used to sleep with the light on in that small room. She's nice. But..."

Clive sipped his beer.

"I must have somebody I can go out with. You know what I mean?"

Remembering, Peter rowed. Daphne reclined in the bow smoking a cigarette. She smiled at him.

"You're humming."

He smiled back.

"I didn't even realize."

"You always hum when you row."

"Do I?"

They both laughed. The rhetorical question was a mannerism of hers.

"It's relaxing," he said.

"Then we must row more often."

"You always say that. But we don't have much time left now."

"No. The season's nearly over."

Between the trees, on both banks, against the foreground of empty chairs, spread over green lawns, they could see a hedge of flowers. Not so long ago people, in shirt sleeves and summer dresses, had sat on the chairs. Children had run on bare feet about them. The white dots of empty deck chairs seemed forlorn now, out of place, gave too strong intimations of an end. Peter rowed. Opposite to him, reclining, Daphne smoked. He rowed slowly, looking at her. She was half-turned away from him and the fingers of one hand were in the water. She seemed relaxed and content.

He had often told himself he ought to hurt her, tell her how much, sometimes, he felt he should resent his gestures, grown so familiar, of his fingers in her hair, of his hand raising the short, cut hair on the nape of her neck or moving over her shoulder. He watched her, smiling, turn to look at him. He ought to provoke and quarrel with her. He was giving too definite shape to the happiness she said he provided. And every day that passed, while he qualified and shaped still more that happiness, made it more difficult, afterwards, as Anna had taught him, for Daphne to find happiness elsewhere.

Rowing, he looked at her. They were in the middle of the pond in a boat become an island for the two of them.

He had escaped, over nearly two years, neither the smell of her hair, the smell of the sweat under her arms, nor even the soured breath from a clogged nose. And the prolonged touch of their aroused bodies becoming normal again together under the blankets was something he had never known in his brief insensitive couplings with Phyllis or in his intense, lustful and brief contacts with Anna.

2

Peter shifted his weight from one leg to the other. It was as if he could see himself and Daphne evoked on the monotonous throb of the liner and reflected in the churned water unravelling perpetually at its stern. It was perhaps a month after their row in the pond that he had awakened, one early Sunday morning, to hear the barely audible notes of the bell of the church at the corner and Daphne crying quietly beside him.

They had talked often about Peter's approaching departure. Daphne had made no reference to herself, left behind in the metropolis, that was not funny. And Peter, laughing, had already been trying to thread his way through the labyrinth of their togetherness back to an original uninvolvement; to feel his way, blinded by the treachery he had not bargained for of their affection, back in time, the thread in his hand, to their decision to live together, make no claims upon each other, to allow either to leave whenever he or she felt like doing so. The noise of her crying, against the background of the barely audible church bells, had surprised him. Behind her facetiousness, behind her oft described reception for him on the island, her imagination peopling it indiscriminately with men in large-brimmed, felt hats and slim-ankled, wide-kneed trousers that blew baggily in a tropical (not metropolitan) wind, with a Guard of Honour standing to attention in the sun under flags, and with groups of women, as he had described them to her, in turbans and ankle-length dresses – behind all, the fantasies and the laughter, her despair had mounted steadily and, that early morning, had overflowed on to his arm.

In the dark, fully awake, the bells stopped now, the clock ticking, he had listened to her. He had given her pleasure and affection in return for all he had taken from her of consolation after Anna had left him. In the dark, he found again his mood of self-indictment, and his assumed exploitation of Daphne loomed more clearly, more accusingly, than his deception of Anna.

He would have liked to hold Daphne close to him; point out, in the dark, the fallacy behind human togetherness; give a lecture, holding her against him on the bed where their bodies had lulled and eventually deceived them, on the instinctual good sense of animals. Or their luck. He wanted to explain the lesson that Anna had taught him – that it was not togetherness but separation, ever present, even from the very beginning, that was real.

He lay in the dark and pretended he was asleep.

He had never let Daphne know he had heard her cry, had submerged his own impotence under a secret and renewed questioning of his responsibility. He forgot he had given her pleasure and he was aware only of the pain he caused now and of the discomfort he might add later to the pain.

Looking down over the rails at the unravelling line of foam, he remembered her funny remarks about people they passed on the streets, her mischievous smile at his embarrassment as, deliberately, exaggeratedly, she hung on his arm. Her playfulness had developed as slowly as their acceptance of each other's nudity in the small bedsitter. But it had exploded almost with the same force of their subsequent lovemaking.

He heard her laughter as he squirmed away from her feet which were always cold, saw the look of innocence that accompanied the cold, plump hand she put under his shirt, heard her imitate the peculiarities he did not always avoid of his island's speech and pronunciation. The line of foam he looked at seemed the only link with the metropolis he had left her in.

But he was glad he had left the city. His private regret for Daphne could not overcome his relief at abandoning a way of life the metropolis had forced upon him. Already, he was aware of an absence of tension and of strain. He had left the city and the special anonymity it conferred behind him. And the unknown woman, who did not know him, but who yet had recognized him sufficiently to whisper her greeting ("I see the niggers are here again") conspiratorially, out of tight lips before the supermarket shelves, would have to look now for others to whisper her special greeting of recognition to. Peter smiled. For a long time he had believed he had remained personally inviolate within the skin he wore which everyone recognized, and that, in the anonymous city, he, too, could have remained anonymous.

He stood in the stern. The water was blue on either side of the churned wake. He was in his shirt sleeves. For two days now, the Atlantic crossing over, the ship had not been out of sight of land. At night it floated, itself alight, on the dark between the lights on islands behind and in front of it. He was almost home; Daphne, far away. But he could, conjure her up, add inches to, or subtract them from her plump thighs, lighten or darken the white flesh of her abdomen. She was more real now than the flesh he had touched; and the voice he heard on the throbbing of the ship was more real than the voice he had listened to. As if, like Anna, Daphne had existed only to leave her image on his mind for him to play with.

He watched the rifling white wake of the ship. By this time tomorrow he would be home. It seemed suddenly to have come very close. It had been for long only a memory, his return to it merely an eventual possibility. His return was fact now. Tomorrow it would become reality.

3

He had refound his apprehension by the time he boarded the small plane that was to take him from the larger island to his own. But the smiles and gestures of surprise when he alighted pleased him. And later, looking out through the window of the taxi that was taking him to the town, everything he saw and heard gave him back his identity, restored perspective and dimension, fixed him in place as well as in time. He saw a tree he had once stoned mangoes from, a house under the raised floor of which he had sheltered from the rain many times as a boy returning from the beach. He went past another, still elegant, old-fashioned and wooden, whose lawns he had not dared to enter. It looked smaller now, less imposing; drab even, he decided in that second's appraisal as he leaned forward to question the neck of the driver he did not know but who had recognized him not, like the woman in the metropolitan supermarket, as part only of a generality, but as a person, the footballer he had been. As he drove along the streets of the town every face he recognized in the sunlight, even of people he had never spoken to, gave him an intense pleasure and satisfaction.

He had got down from the car at the entrance to a dirty block of flats, built after the fire, and, with his single small suitcase, climbed dirty, concrete steps and walked along a dirty verandah to peep through the glass pane of the kitchen window. His mother looked up to see what had caused the shadow then rushed to open the door and to cling to him on the verandah, the noise of the Electric Power Station and of traffic from the streets about the two of them, holding him as if to make up in her embrace for the absence of contact his non-writing had been, looking up into his face, the tears coming to her eyes. As she held him silently, he heard the familiar roar from the market place, the familiar beat of the Station engines, the noises from the street, and smiled upon the grey in the hair which was all that he could see now as, her face buried in his abdomen, she recited the "*Magnificat Anima Mea Dominum*".

She took him inside, her prayers over, laughing and crying. The room seemed smaller; the pictures on the walls, framed in *passepartout*, more numerous than he remembered them. He saw forgotten pictures of Paul and himself in the school team, a new picture of his father standing, in his new uniform, next to his new car; the picture of Phyllis and himself taken the day of their wedding and, separately, in identical poses, each on his belly on a towel, his two children, both dead, the twins he had never seen.

And then the church bells rang out the Angelus. His mother crossed herself and began the prayers aloud. Peter smiled and did not respond. She continued her prayers quietly and alone. The bells were pealing. They filled the room with their sound. Once they had been the signal that it was time for lunch. No matter where he had been in this small town, or even on the edges of it, he had heard those bells. His mother had finished praying.

"So you don't pray any more?"

The bells had stopped. Only the increased noises of cars and of people walking home to lunch from work came through the open window. He heard the shouts of children going home from school. His mother put on a hat, took a basket from the kitchen, and went out. Peter walked to the small private verandah on the other side of the building. He had to squint for the sun. And the children he looked at, the heat that rose from the streets, the bells he had heard, reminded him of his own schooldays. Now and then, out of a passing car, an astonished hand waved at him. His mother joined him. There was a bottle of rum in the basket.

"For your friends," she said, "when they come."

He followed her back into the room and poured himself a drink. Then while she went to prepare lunch in the kitchen, he sat in the bright light of the verandah.

Michael came home first from school. His grandmother followed him to the verandah.

"You know this gentleman?"

Michael looked at his uncle and smiled. He was tall and resembled his mother.

"You don't know him?"

His voice, thin too, was like his mother's.

"I know."

"Well, who then?"

"Is Uncle Peter."

They shook hands. His grandmother returned to the kitchen. Phyllis came in while Peter was talking to his nephew. Husband and wife kissed. It was like kissing Daphne goodbye before she went to work. Then Paul arrived. The brothers shook hands. There was neither fuss nor excitement. Their mother had been laying the table. They were all, the four of them, going to eat together.

She apologized for lunch. It was Peter's fault if there was nothing special. He should have written. She came and went with the dishes for which there was not space on the narrow table.

"You never like to write," she told Peter.

She encouraged Michael who, alone, seemed completely unaffected, to relate for Peter some of the stories he was always telling her.

"He always telling stories. But he don't know how to add."

Michael made a face and looked even more like his mother. Under the narrow table, Peter's and Phyllis's knees touched.

"Staying long?" Paul asked.

"A week."

"Eh, eh," Michael said, "only a week?" His thin voice sang out the sentence.

"Your uncle don't like to write," Peter's mother said. Phyllis was quiet.

"You just come and you going awready?" Michael said.

Peter nodded.

"Eh, eh."

The others were eating silently. His mother standing near the table was sipping from a glass. She alone was sharing the rum with Peter. After every sip she made a noise with her tongue against her palate. Peter affected relish for the food and drank much. But he was uncomfortable and felt better only when the others had gone out again and he was sitting alone on the verandah. He could hear his mother washing up in the kitchen and, from over the verandah rails, the noises, increased again, of cars, of clerks returning to work and of children going noisily back to school. Every now and then, her hands covered with soapsuds, his mother joined him on the verandah to make a comment or to ask a question. He was drowsy from the heat and his drinking. After a while the streets became relatively quiet again. The shouts of children ceased. The beat of the Power Station reminded him of the throb of the ship. His mother, her hands dried now, joined him on the verandah.

She had changed much from the woman who once had stood, her hands on her hips, supervising the beating Paul administered to him. Or, and Peter smiled, the woman who had beaten Paul ("you older, you should know better") every time he and Paul fought, no matter how much Peter had provoked him.

She told him Paul was in charge of a warehouse. Nothing had changed. Paul and his father still did not speak to each other.

"Is only quarrel they don't quarrel any more," she said.

Peter and his brother had never got together after the fight in which Peter had chased Paul with a knife. Paul had cornered him. He had learnt not to be provoked by Peter's taunts to fight in the presence of their parents. Their last fight, the cause of which Peter no longer remembered, had taken place when they were alone. Neither had mentioned it. And Peter, fearing reprisal, had avoided his brother, even when they were not alone, until it had become habit for him to do so. After Peter, too, had won a scholarship to St Mary's College, their mother had tried to get them to do their homework together. Paul was impatient with him, called him a dunce, told him he had no discipline. Peter resented it. Soon they were doing their homework silently each at one end of the narrow table, the oil lamp on its centre.

Disciplined Paul certainly had been. He studied hard, topped his class. He became a superb batsman. He practised in the yard at the back of the house, using a broomstick as a bat and playing the stockinged ball that hung from a branch almost at his shin, his body bent well forward. When he played it was not easy to get him out. At football he did not score goals. Paul did not like to jostle or be jostled. He made goals. He deceived and displaced the opposition and created gaps for his team mates to exploit.

In time, Peter, too, had become a member of the school's soccer team. But his play, effective, too, was not as controlled as Paul's. Peter had not altogether lost the influence of the boys he had played with on the wharf and who were porters and stevedores now. It was from them that he had learnt to reach for the knife and, later, to throw a boy twice his height to daze him by the fall on his head. He became excited when he played.

Paul never was. And it was Paul that his former friends talked about, standing for hours in a circle near the wharf and the market, waiting for jobs, juggling and keeping in the air with their bare feet, often for as many as a hundred times without its touching the ground, a dried orange or a rotten lime.

Paul alone seemed not to be affected by what was said or written about him. But he practised assiduously in the yard, alone, in long spells. He skipped until his body dripped with sweat and his light blue trunks were discoloured by the liquid that had soaked through them.

Peter listened to his mother. Her concern, which she tried to hide, showed. She was worried about Paul, about Michael, about Peter and Phyllis. Peter allowed her to talk.

Perhaps Paul had inherited their father's propensity for appearances, for making the gesture calculated to impress and, if necessary, deceive the public. Their mother having to stop selling ground provisions in the market had been such a gesture. The buying of the house, soon to be destroyed, uninsured, by fire, another. Their father, repressing his stammer, had never spoken much. But Peter and his brother had often, during those months that followed the buying of the house, heard their mother say, "People think we rich; we don't have to tell them no. And nobody don't have to know what we eating in the house, even if is dirt. I talking to you, Peter. Is you especially I talking to, because you have all those friends on the wharf to tell them your family business."

Always she had supported her husband, accepting his leadership, must have done so ever since, at eighteen, she had followed him from the small coastal village to the capital where he became a warder. And Paul's had been the only note of opposition that Peter had heard sounded. That voice, raised not only for the first time but also with an extreme vehemence, he had not forgotten. From the table where he was eating Peter had watched and listened, pretending not to, quietly, uninvolved. He saw his mother hold back her husband. It was the first gesture unconnected with giving or receiving, of food or of money, that he had seen between his parents. He had never heard a word of tenderness between them, had surprised no look or touch of affection. And her acceptance of his authority had never given him cause to hit her.

She was talking still, next to him on the verandah, this time about matters he hardly bothered to listen to. He put a hand around her shoulders. Like her, Phyllis had received no gestures of affection from her husband. It was to Anna, and to Daphne, that he had made them.

But marriage, he told himself, removing his hand from her shoulder, was only a word. He sipped his rum, closed his eyes. A gesture that, like so many others, they had imitated. He sipped his drink again. His marriage rattled in his unsober mind like cans on a cat's tail. The sounds it made were mingled with the increased sounds he heard from the market and the Power Station on the other side of the building.

"Your father."

The sounds from the market and the Power Station were muted again. His mother was standing and watching him closely, it seemed. Peter pulled himself together as his father appeared on the verandah, heard his father's "What?" of surprise, saw his father's face break into a smile, felt the handshake and the touch of his father's lips on his lowered cheek. He was surprised less by the elegant, unfamiliar Superintendent's uniform than by the new intimacy of his father's kiss and the totally bald head that the older man had uncovered. Peter bent down to kiss it. They laughed.

4

The two men drank together for the first time, not on the verandah but inside, sitting at the table where his father was about to eat. Success had made them friends. His father talked about the bungalow he hoped to move to in the hills on the town's edge. And when he put on his cap again and went out to buy another bottle of rum, Peter followed him to the long, communal verandah to look down at the new car. Inside again, he went into the kitchen. His mother was happy. He could see that. He reached for a piece of yam she had already prepared for her husband and put it in his mouth.

"You still have your bad manners."

She took a piece of meat from the prepared dish and gave it to him.

"Take it."

As his mouth closed about the meat, his lips brushing the tips of her fingers, it seemed for a moment, absurdly, that the present, the interval of his absence cut away, had rejoined the past. He watched her preparing his father's meal. Her dress hung inelegantly, quaint and unadorned. Her greying hair was short, almost as short as his own. Chewing the meat she had given him, he was unable not to have images of her in a past the feel of her fingers on his lips had evoked.

She had tried at first to speak to Paul. Laughing

hollowly and touching his head she told him it would make him mad to think so much. She made excuses for her husband. Peter had watched and listened, always pretending he was not doing either. At first Paul was silent. Then he chased her. Her laughter had grated with what Peter had discovered in it of bewildered pain. She pushed Paul's head again, concealing her anxiety with rills of a gaiety she could not have felt. Paul flared angrily and moved away. And she had watched him, after that, from a distance only.

In the kitchen now, she seemed content. But she had never railed against an unforgiving husband, a frightened, disillusioned son, an unresponsive God. Peter was not fooled by her quiet. He could estimate the extent of her happiness for him, for the reconciliation with his father; estimate, too, the pain her comparison caused between himself and Paul.

The noise of the Power Station was loud again, briefly. His father had returned. He invited Peter to eat. They had never eaten together. And it was of a past, which they had not shared, that they talked while they ate. The present was with them and, for the older man, the future was contained now in it. The car outside was present and future; the new furniture, the refrigerator, the bungalow he was going to put them in. The future, for long only possibility, was tangible, visible. The possibility and the event were fused. And so, they talked about the past.

Peter spoke about the reflection of his face in his father's boots as he shone them, his walks with food to the prison barracks. His father told him the names of his former friends who had been to gaol. He had often beaten Peter for playing with them. They talked about the beatings they could remember. His mother, sucking a bone as she stood near the table, laughed with them at their recollections.

And then Peter laughed and laughed. He reminded his father of the beating he had given Peter one Christmas, one of the worst beatings he had received.

"I remember that well," his mother said. "You went after the Devil and you didn't come back till after six. You spent the whole day in the street."

Peter felt again his fear of the monster that so attracted him, saw himself running with other boys as the Devil charged with his fork, frothing at the mouth, shaking his head and grinding out frightful noises of anger. Once he had dared to creep up behind the fire-eating figure to pull its tail, had been terrified by the sudden, unexpected turn of the mask, had himself turned and run, hearing the fall of feet behind him, had run, he told his parents, more than he had ever run before, or since, he believed, and had turned, running still and hearing the feet that followed, to discover he had been running all the time alone, pursued by no sound of feet except the ones he heard in his mind.

His parents laughed.

"He was running after another boy who had burst a firecracker just as he turned to look at me."

"Paul never liked the masquerade, you know," his mother said.

It was the first mention of Paul's name, the first allowance that, in that past they were evoking, Paul, too, had existed.

"And the thing is," Peter said, "I knew all the time that it was Julien, the fisherman, who was behind the mask."

"He's dead now, you know."

It was the devil he saw that he had run away from, not the fisherman he knew behind the mask; the devil who pursued you and prodded with his wooden fork, in spite of your cries, prodded when you had no place to flee to, caught against the wooden fence at the end of a yard, prodded with the devil's roar, not the fisherman's voice, prodded, hurt, frightened you into an acceptance of his make-believe...

Peter realized his father, too, was laughing a great deal. He did not remember what funny episode he had just brought up from the past. He did not stop laughing. The meal was over. He and his father moved away from the table. But they had never talked, his father and himself, any more than he and Paul had talked. And when they had exhausted their memories, they found they had little else to say to each other.

5

That night, after eight years, he lay again in the same bed with Phyllis. He had drunk much. The news of his unexpected arrival had spread in the small town and after work his friends had come to see him. They sat on the verandah. Every now and then some one had gone out and returned with a bottle. Phyllis came from work and went out again with Michael. Paul was working late, his mother told him. It was something that happened often. As he drank and laughed with his friends Peter looked over the rails of the verandah at the hills. It seemed they had never been so green nor so close. It had been adventure, once, for him to get among the mangoes and guavas on them.

His friends had changed – in ways, sometimes, he could not have expected. It was not only the wives and the children they spoke about with such intimacy to him who knew only some of the people they mentioned and none of the children, nor the manner in which the jobs they now held on the island had qualified their attitudes to one another. Almost all of them worked in the Civil Service. They made references to things he did not understand, could not have known anything of. And, in one or two instances, physical appearances had changed so much that he would not have easily recognized, in the person he looked at now, the other, purportedly the same, he had left behind. And so, listening to them and looking at the hills, he was aware of a sense of flux, of change and motion. And it was for this reason that he continued, sitting and drinking with his friends, and looking at the hills, to think of his father. His father's implacably sustained resentment against Paul reminded Peter of Duncan's.

It might have been Peter's father who, facing him across the table of the pub and showing strong traces of their island's speech beneath his newly acquired, metropolitan accent, had said,

"I resent the fucker because he might have provided and he didn't."

Duncan unbuttoned his bus conductor's jacket. There was very little to differentiate him from the metropolitans sitting about them. His conductor's cap was on his head.

"My father was irresponsible," he added. "He was a fucking hypocrite. He was running with the hare and hunting with the bloody hounds. You know what he told me once?"

"What?" Peter asked.

"I was a little boy at the time, but I'll never forget it. We were going for a walk. He always used to take me with him for walks on the estate on mornings. He used to say I was his favourite."

Peter, sipping his beer, had pictured Phyllis on the estate, walking in the early morning with Duncan, their hands in their father's.

"Favourite my arsehole."

Duncan had spat out the words. People in the pub turned to look at him.

"He was angry that morning. We passed the overseer. I said '*Bonjour M'sieu Flan*' as usual. I always called the old man *M'sieu*. But my father was angry. So you know what he said to me? He says, 'Don't ever let me hear you call a black man *Mister* again.' He said that. To me."

He sipped his beer. Peter had understood his resentment. Duncan had awakened one day to find that his father had died suddenly, his mother become destitute, his world of privilege, once so real, effaced forever. For Peter's father privilege had been only vision, the vision of his sons', and of his own future achievement. And, like Duncan locked up with his resentment in a memory his father's death had imprisoned him in, Peter's father was still chained to the vision he had glimpsed and the end he imagined Paul had threatened to bring to it. It might have been he, not Duncan, dressed in a bus conductor's winter uniform, who carried memories of a childhood paradise as he waited, his hand over the cord, to ring the bell for the bus to move on again.

Peter lay next to Phyllis. He had often, especially after he had met Anna, wondered how much marriage to him had been part of Phyllis's attempt to escape from the net that Old Desmangues, by his sudden death, had spun for his illegitimate children.

"I don't want an abortion. You don't have to marry me if you don't want to."

But she must have known that, after what had happened with Paul, he had no choice. Neither his threats, his pleadings, had been able to make her change her mind. The day of the wedding his father worked all day.

Her mother and her brothers did not attend. Paul was at work. It was September. Three weeks later, on a scholarship he had so much feared they might have withdrawn, he went to study at the university on the larger island to the north.

To him on it his mother wrote that his father had become deputy Chief Warder and urged, for a long time in vain, that Peter write to him. It was she who told him that the children had been born, that they had died, that their mother had been seriously ill.

It had been like receiving messages from a hilltop in semaphore. His children were no more than images on a piece of cardboard. Waiting for their birth had been like watching the notice board to read the names of finalists he did not know. Phyllis and her illness were as unreal as the names he read that conjured up no individuals for him. And the unreality of distance had been heightened by the unreality in time. She was already well again, and the twins long dead, when his mother had thought it safe to write to him. After his own finals, he did not return, even briefly, to his island home. He made excuses, pretended regret and promised to send for Phyllis once he was settled in Europe. His plans remained plans. He met Anna in the metropolis three months after he had come to it.

Peter opened his eyes in the dark. He was aware of the bulge of Phyllis's body without turning to look at it, the outline, in the flesh, of the outline she had for so long only been.

"Are you asleep?"

"No."

"It's late!"

"I know."

He had not been willing to come to her. And he had been pleased to talk to Paul on the verandah, unexpectedly, after the last of his friends had long gone and he was still hesitating by himself over a glass of rum and ice. Empty bottles and a bowl of ice were at his feet. The street lights he looked at over the verandah rails were like sentinels.

"I must congratulate you."

"Thanks."

"Have a drink?" Peter asked, in order to break the pause.

"You know I don't drink."

"A little one. To celebrate."

"Celebrate what?"

Peter did not know.

"Our reunion," he said.

Paul laughed.

"We're too old," he said.

"What do you mean?"

"We're a little old to pretend."

Peter felt uncomfortable. It was like the times when, away from their parents, Paul used to corner him.

"I suppose we are, Paul."

Paul's directness had antagonized him.

"To celebrate my success then. Perhaps your father's."

"That's fair."

The Power Station's engines throbbed steadily. An absence of heat on the verandah was not yet, however, coolness.

"Your father must be pleased."

"Yes, I think he was."

"He can afford to be expansive now."

Peter was beginning to fall asleep, lulled by the drink and by the beat of the engines which so much resembled that of the ship. He leaned against the back of his chair, his eyes closed.

"I hear you're now in charge of the warehouse," he said.

"Yes. I, too, have been promoted." Paul smiled.

Peter did not see it. He was dozing.

"You'd better go to sleep," he heard.

"Sorry," he said. "Tired. A little drunk. Sorry."

He stood up, held on to the verandah rails and breathed in deeply once or twice. After the last inhalation he felt the sense of touch almost leave his fingers clenched over the metal rail. He was afraid he might fall. A second later he was all right again, hearing no more the pounding in his ears but the controlled throb of the Power Station.

"Let's go for a walk," he said.

"I thought you were sleeping."

"I'm awake now."

He stretched. He wished he could put off indefinitely his meeting with Phyllis.

6

He lay next to Phyllis. The ceiling he looked at, unlike the one he had looked at as a boy, of the house that had been burnt, was flat and formed no apex for bats to appropriate and hang upside down from. On early mornings, sometimes, he used to see them outlined briefly against the open window, wings outspread, and he had marvelled once at the length of tooth and span of wing of one he had killed. He had thought the creature ugly, reprehensible, had queried an existence that had allowed it to hang from the dark apex of the roof during the day and fly out into the dark at night. One night of the week that followed Anna's departure, lying on his bed in the heated bedsitter, he had suddenly heard the high-pitched squeal as though the sound he remembered were in the hot lighted room, uttered by himself who flitted out, sustained by the wings of his scholarship and a fear of returning to the island, to bite in libraries at bits of information and, at night, flitted in again to the room that he had appropriated temporarily in the alien metropolis.

After his short walk with Paul, unwilling still to join Phyllis, he had resumed his drinking amid the chaos of bottles on the floor of the verandah, sitting in a night, alone, that for the first time was cool.

He looked at the flat ceiling. Out of the corner of his

eye he made out her shape. The room seemed to tremble faintly on the beat of the station engines. He resented the assurance with which, over eight years, Phyllis had waited for him. Their intimacy had not stretched much beyond a few minutes in the yard, in an empty room, occasionally, on the beach. Even after their marriage, when they had spent entire nights together, they had not been more prolongedly intimate. After eight years, she had no smell for him to evoke, no gesture for him to remember. It was a stranger he had returned to. And the reminder of his expediency.

He lay next to it. For years Phyllis had been no more than the picture which, with that of the twins, Anna had surprised between the pages of one of his books. No. That was not quite true. She had already existed, as an obstacle, that night when he returned with the bottle of wine to the bedsitter and saw Anna with the picture and the inscription *To my dear Husband* in Phyllis's copperplate at the back of it.

He shifted on the bed.

It had been the delightful Anna who had surprised him with her weekend bag earlier that evening: the Anna who made him think of the little girl she might have been, running over the lawn, pursued by a nurse in a white apron; the adolescent Anna, as he imagined her, playing for her mother on the piano; the Anna he had seen, listening to her, riding with other school girls on bicycles along the esplanade near the sea front; the Anna that gave him so much pleasure, who blinded him to the contradictions of the unbeautiful, graceful girl she was, whom he would have liked to own – it had been she who, waltzing over the limited space of his small bedsitter, had said it was her surprise, that it was her birthday, and that she had come of age.

She had been calm, listening to his explanation, her things on the bed, her empty bag beside them. Before he had finished she was putting the things back again into it. He had made no attempt to stop her and, afterwards, had lain on the bed, alone, looking silently at the possibility that might have preserved her for him. Then he had drunk the wine.

Peter sat up on the edge of the bed. Phyllis stirred. Peter stood up.

"What're you doing?"

"I'm not sleepy."

He went back to the last of the rum on the verandah, going carefully down the stairs, not putting on any light.

He might have known she would follow him. Affecting politeness he asked whether she would not be too tired for work the next day.

"No."

She sat next to him. He resented her now as he had not during all the years he had been avoiding her. It was the authority of her clothed body next to his, its affirmation (in her breathing and her warmth) of her real existence that made him purse his lips in the light on the verandah which was too faint, he was glad, for her to notice. Even as an obstacle she had existed only in the abstract, removed in time as well as in space.

"What's the matter?" she asked.

He put a hand unsoberly on her neck and felt the strangeness of her uncut, mulatto hair.

"You'd better go to bed."

"Have I done something?"

He resented her humility, her apparent readiness to assume blame. Already, like Daphne's worrying when his work went badly, her assumption of blame had brought her closer to him.

"Don't be silly."

"I'm sorry."

It seemed an apology, full of sarcasm, for something she knew she did not deserve to be blamed for. He felt she was mocking, laughing at, him.

"You'd better go to bed."

She did not move. He watched her indistinctness close to him. She had not travelled to another part of the world, had not followed any paths of specialized knowledge, knew no sun that was not hot; she had not discovered, in herself or in others, human deceit and cynicism, had never known the delights of intimate human togetherness. She had remained in her world, been formed only by it, had waited in it with a confidence he found at once insolent and accusing, with a patience he could not help being flattered by. He understood. If, for Anna's sake, he had wished Phyllis had never been, Phyllis, now, could only wish he would always be.

"Go on."

Her refusal irritated him. He knew she must be confused and pained. That, for her, who had held to him for years in her imagination only and, by proxy, in the occasional letters she received, in his parents' house which was the only home she possessed on the island, it must be impossible she should not continue to hold on, perhaps even more desperately, now. But he did not dwell on her confusion or on her pain. Only a single-mindedness, remembered, construed already as design, remained for him to dwell upon.

"Phyllis."

"Yes, Ma."

"Come back here."

"Yes, Ma."

"This minute."

She and her brothers, already, had had to leave secondary school. Where once old Desmangues had sat, next to the half-opened window, her mother argued now, late on Saturday nights, in her nightgown, with those people who had rented the large unsuccessful café to hold a dance and wished to prolong it. One of the wooden supports of the verandah had fallen and, in rooms above the cafe, prostitutes entertained the white sailors of ships that were in the harbour.

"Come inside, I say. You don't have no shame!"

Peter's father, beating him for playing with "Wharf-rats" had used the same words to him. For Phyllis's family, insecurity had replaced the assurance that old Desmangues, alive, had provided. More supports had fallen. The verandah sagged dangerously.

"You don't have no shame. Is those same people talking and laughing behind your back."

Shame, for long not even a possibility, had become real now.

"Is you going to be next. Is you they going to make pregnant and kill herself."

Phyllis had not ceased to come. She talked to him about the sagging verandah, the dances that went on and on and on on Saturday nights, the rooms upstairs when the ships were in. Her brothers had already fled the island. Duncan worked on the cable ship which remained at sea for as many as six months at a time. Phyllis worked in a store, was taking lessons in stenography. She came, read his books and still spoke of convent as a later possibility. Her former friends were now in the higher forms there.

"I won't have an abortion. You don't have to marry me if you don't want to."

Her remembered single-mindedness, the tears forgotten now that had accompanied it, angered him. "Didn't you hear?"

She sat, said nothing and did not move. Peter drank the rum in his glass and walked back to their room upstairs. He did not hear her follow him. And the next morning, when he awoke, late, Phyllis, already had left for work.

7

The sun was up. He saw spots in the ceiling he had not noticed the night before. But he remembered them. They had been there before he left the island. He had come back, rejoined a past he had deliberately not looked at for eight years. Even the birthday and Christmas cards he had received from Phyllis he had resented. On the island where he was an undergraduate, time and distance had already put a hood over his emotions. In the metropolis, he had closed his eyes behind the slits of that hood.

It was Anna who, departed, had animated what had been only an occasional memory to forget, an image on cardboard to be hidden between the pages of a book, the grammatical mistakes in elegant copperplate on Air Mail paper to be torn and flushed down the toilet. She had already fleshed that image with Peter's regret for the obstacle Phyllis had become. Her departure, making him construe Phyllis's tearful decision not to abort as plan, breathed into the recreated flesh and blood, cunning and deceit.

He sat on the edge of the bed. Through the half-opened door of the small wardrobe that had not been there before he left the island he saw bits of Phyllis's dresses, a belt on the floor, a white shoe. The small bookshelf he had himself made of boxwood was painted now. The books on it seemed undisturbed. He wondered how much and what Phyllis read. In the old days he had been pleased to watch her read his school books and to wonder, looking at her mulatto skin, and without any real intent, what their children would look like.

He would never be sure how much her complexion had added to the flattery of her continuing, despite her mother's warnings, to visit him.

He dressed and went downstairs. He was alone in the house. He found strong, black coffee kept warm against the coalpot, waiting for him in the kitchen. The bottles he had left on the verandah stood together in a corner. While he was drinking the coffee, his mother returned.

"Morning," she said.

"Morning, Ma."

"Is so you used to drink where you was?"

"No. Yesterday was special."

"And you didn't even go to church this morning."

How little, for her, he must have changed! He thought of things she would not have understood and would have been pained to know he had done.

"It woulda been so nice for you and Phyllis to go?"

He might never have left the island, been locked up on it, in a time that had not evolved. He looked at her wide-brimmed hat, the dress that came down almost to the ankles. She wore stockings. She, too, had gone to church. Perhaps together with Phyllis. He wondered what Phyllis had prayed for.

"The news in the papers. Everybody giving me *Bonne Fête*."

Paul, too, had once, been news. Everything in this small town became news.

"You must go and see —— and ——." She listed

people, friends and former neighbours, she would like him to visit.

"Your godmother was always asking about you."

It was from his godmother, a seamstress, that he had received the black thread and the pins which he bent into hooks to fish with from the wharf's edge.

"I don't know if I ever told you. —— is dead. And ——."

Peter listened to names of people who had died and whom he could not remember.

"I bring a paper for you."

And before he had finished reading the newspaper she had handed him, she asked, "You hungry?"

"Yes."

She produced roasted salt cod in olive oil with pepper and chipped raw onion, lettuce and avocado pear. It was a surprise.

"I know you used to like it."

The bread was stale. She had not forgotten that he had liked bread which had become stale in a closed bin.

"I tried to get a lobster. But you can't get it these days. The fishermen selling all to the hotels. They does pay them more. Even if you lucky enough sometimes to get one, is a small one the hotels don't want. And you have to pay so much now for it."

"It's all right, Ma."

"You don't like to write." He had heard her say that the day before.

"I'll write," he said, "I promise."

"What about Phyllis, you taking her with you?"

"I'll send for her."

"Again?"

"It won't take so long this time. This is nice, Ma. You know how much a pear cost in Europe?"

"She's done a lot for Michael."

He did not want to hear of her virtues. Too completely, they seemed to implicate him in a decision she alone had made. But he ate and listened. Before he got up to go out, he told her, "This time, I'll send for her as soon as I get there."

8

He had no place to go to. He walked slowly along the street past the overflow of vendors from the market, their fruit and vegetables laid out on crocus bags spread out on the pavement before them. The faces he looked at were unfamiliar. He did not find again the excitement of his drive in the taxi yesterday from the airport to the town. His friends were at work. His mother's friends would be already in the markets buying the day's lunch. The people he went past did not know him: he did not know them. He noticed some berries he remembered he had liked and stopped to buy a few. He was surprised how much the price had increased.

But, as he ate them, walking aimlessly, the berries conjured for him, suddenly, an adolescent world of half-Indian, half-Negro girls coming daily from the hills to sell milk out of kerosene tins which they carried in small wooden trays on their heads. They brought whatever fruit was in season as gifts for himself and Paul and the purple berries, whose patois names he had forgotten and whose English ones he had never known, had been among the gifts the girls brought.

It was in the rainy season that he saw the sisters now, the elder, tall and straight, the younger, short and acquiring already the round plumpness of her Negro mother. Their wet dresses stuck to their brown bodies, outlining their pants. Their bare feet were wrinkled and very white at the toes and at the edges of the soles. Laughing, they stood in the kitchen and sipped hot coffee his mother had given them. Peter saw their shivering bodies, heard their laughter clearly, evoked by the berries, more clearly than he had seen them in memory when, unexpectedly, in one of the metropolitan streets, he had met the older one outside of a supermarket, her overcoat covering all of the body that her wet, clinging dress had allowed him to see.

Her presence, and her transformation, in that city had surprised him. She told him, laughing, in English he could barely understand, that she had been in it for six years. She had come with her husband. She was working in a factory. He spoke to her in patois, pretending that it suited their unexpected meeting in the strange city. After she left he had turned to look at her. Below her coat, standing out of her shoes, her stockinged legs showed. Her shod gait, even after six years, was inelegant and, like the language she spoke, uncertain. She disappeared into the crowd.

Aimlessly, he walked through the noise and bustle of the market place, his mind full of the world of his berries, his mouth of their taste, his fingers stained with the purple of their flesh.

"Peter."

He turned. Colin was emerging from a large American car. They had last seen each other in the metropolis where Colin was studying Law.

"Well, well, well." Colin was laughing. "I was just thinking of coming to see you."

They shook hands.

"I've only just read the news. I was in the country yesterday with some cases and came back late. Got up late too." He pointed to his sports shirt and his shorts. "I'm resting this morning. Mustn't work too hard, you know." He grinned. "So how, man?"

They stood on the pavement for a while.

"Look, what you doing?"

"Nothing."

"How about a drive, then? I was waiting to take Bertha back to the house, that's our servant, but she can walk."

"I'd like a drive, yes."

"Come on."

They entered the car.

"How's Helen?"

"All right. Working hard like hell. You know those English girls already. Trying to be independent."

They were moving slowly along the narrow right-angled streets of the town. Colin blew the horn of the big car often.

"Children?"

Colin smiled. Peter remembered that smile from their school days. It was the smile Colin used when he was out at cricket for a low score and was returning to the pavilion or when he could not substantiate a boast that he had made.

"No, boy," he said, "not yet."

They were soon in the hills. The car sped easily up them. Colin pointed to the dashboard.

"Like it?" He smiled. "Got it cheap. From a grateful client. An American who was in some trouble. Guess how much I paid?"

"Don't know."

"Guess."

And he told Peter.

"Next to nothing," he added.

They stopped at his home among the new concrete

and glass bungalows with lawns and dogs that barked from behind fences.

"Helen's at work. We can go in for a drink."

"Not now," Peter said, "I think I'd prefer a drive."

They drove back to the main road.

"You must come and eat with us. How long you're here for?"

"A week."

"Boy," Colin prolonged the word. And then, "What about tomorrow?"

They had come to the flat stretch of road that ran parallel to the coast for miles.

"Look!"

They were travelling at over eighty miles per hour.

"And you can hardly feel anything," Colin said.

The big car was slowing down. The road was soon going to begin again to climb and turn.

"I just remembered," Colin said. "I have to go to —— tomorrow. I may not be back from court there in time. We'll have to make it the day after. We're having Sydney and his wife to dinner. You remember Sydney?"

"Yes. I think that'd be all right."

"I'll pick you and Phyllis at seven the day after to morrow. How's that?"

"Fine."

"How's Anna?"

"She's all right."

"Has she gone back? Or is she still in the city?"

"She's gone back."

"That was a nice girl, boy."

"Yes."

They drove uphill.

"I'd like to come to —— with you tomorrow."

"Good idea. I'll pick you up at six-thirty in the morning. You think you'll be up?"

"I don't see why not."

"I know why," Colin said. "I've only been to see your mother once since I came back."

He laughed.

"You heard about the big hotel they've built near La Colombe?"

"Yes. Are we going there?"

Colin nodded.

"You won't recognize the place."

They drove on.

"Phyllis looking well, man."

"Yes."

"You're a damn lucky fellow, you know, Peter."

Peter smiled.

"You've had the best of two worlds."

Peter smiled.

"You scamp," Colin grinned. "You're not even defending yourself."

And a little later,

"Do you correspond, you and Anna?"

Peter shook his head.

"You dropped her just like that."

"There's nothing else I can do, is there?"

"I suppose not. She didn't find out about Phyllis?"

"No."

"Boy, I'd like to know how you managed that. You know, I can't make a move here without Helen knowing. And you know she doesn't even try to find out things. People just come and tell her. Wives of friends." He sucked his teeth amiably. "Give me the city every time," he said.

They sat outside of the hotel in the shade of an

umbrella and watched the sea. Only a few people were about.

"It's the slack season now," Colin said.

They drank brandy and ginger and talked desultorily against the background of the noise of small waves.

"We'd better eat, eh?" Colin said.

Colin ate steak with potatoes, lettuce and tomatoes. It was all, he said, imported from America.

"Even the man who cooked it," he said.

Peter noted to himself that he would after all be able to tell his mother that he had eaten lobster for lunch.

9

Phyllis was gone again the next morning (to Mass this time, it was too early for work) when Peter awoke and began to get ready for his drive to —— with Colin. He heard Paul leave his bedroom and walk down the stairs. Then he heard the increased noises from outside as his brother went out of the front door. A little later Michael knocked on his door.

"Come in."

Michael entered with a cup of coffee.

"Morning, Uncle."

"Morning, Michael."

"Granny say to bring your coffee for you if you get up."

"Thanks."

"She gone to church with Aunty Phyllis. She say if it not sweet enough I must bring more sugar."

Peter sipped the coffee.

"It's sweet enough," he said, "but it's very hot."

"That? Very hot? I does drink hotter coffee than that, *oui*."

Peter was irritated by his nephew's language as he had been by Phyllis's the night before. But, again, he said nothing. Michael's language was no different from what his must have been. He imagined the rebuke his own father would have administered, backed perhaps by a slap or a blow on the head, for the unseamed shorts, the crumpled shirt, the unshone shoes with the turned-up tips. Peter glimpsed neglect, perhaps indifference.

"You not going to church?" Michael asked.

"No."

"Eh, eh. God will punish you."

Peter smiled.

"You not afraid?"

"No."

"Eh, eh."

Peter sipped his coffee.

"You'll go to hell when you die, you'll see."

Peter said nothing.

"You playing bad, eh?"

And Peter laughed. He had glimpsed neglect. He listened to innocence.

"And you, aren't you going?"

"Of course. I does go to Mass every morning."

Michael sang out the words in a manner Peter had long forgotten.

"You'll be late, then."

Michael looked at Phyllis's clock.

"No. You trying to fool me. It only five to seven. You think I don' know time?"

"Who taught you?"

"Aunty Phyllis."

He skipped out of the room.

Colin blew the horn of his car a short while later. Outside, the sun threw long slanted shadows of everything he looked at. The stores and shops were still closed. The streets were still relatively empty. In a short time he and Colin were at the edge of the town. In the hills, along the narrow, climbing road, the big car moved slowly and with difficulty. More than once Colin had to reverse and complete hairpin bends in two movements. Conversation, under the circumstances was desultory. Colin gave much attention to driving and there were long silences, welcomed by Peter, as he looked out at the countryside. This time, however, he kept the excitement of his rediscovery in perspective, so much so that, in a few minutes, what he saw served only as a background against which his thoughts, of himself and Phyllis the night before, moved with him.

Colin had brought him home late from the hotel where they had had lunch. His mother had complained. She had herself prepared lunch for him and it was cold. Before he went out again, this time to visit his godmother and some of the people she had asked him to visit, Peter had promised to come home in time for dinner. He had been only a little late. Phyllis, who had been waiting, ate with him. His mother, standing near the table and talking to them, would not have guessed at the incident that had taken place on the verandah. He had watched the manner in which Phyllis held her fork, her little finger sticking out; listened to the English she spoke, her "*ouis*" and her "*nons*" at the end of her sentences.

After the meal his mother (and Michael) had sat with them on the verandah. When they left (his mother dragging an unwilling Michael off with her), it was to still the increasing restlessness and confusion of his thoughts, his inner contradictions, that Peter had suggested a drink.

Phyllis immediately offered to get it. Peter began to refuse, stopped, remembering the night before, and stood up to get money from his trousers' pocket. Phyllis turned away, neglecting the money, adding thus to her service the gift of her offering. He had been at once hurt and moved that she had brought back the most expensive brand of whiskey for him. He drank copiously, drowning his ambivalence, while he told her of Duncan and their infrequent meetings in the metropolis. And that night, after he had lain on the bed for some minutes, convinced that he was melodramatic not to touch her, he had finally turned to that body which did not attract him, his lust aroused, and mounted it. The ease of coitus when he had not prepared her for it did not surprise him. And the night broken for them now by their breathing as well as the discreet steady throb of the Power Station engines, he had lain upon her unloved, responsive flesh, her body moving beneath him and the pressure of her arms locked at the back of his shoulders testifying to the willingness with which she had received him.

How long after that lustful coupling he remained awake, he did not remember. He lay on his back, prised away from contact with her not only by their perspiration and the heat their bodies had generated but also, his lust assuaged, by a sense of his own dishonesty.

"Taking it all in?" Colin asked.

Peter smiled, looking out of the window.

"I know the feeling," Colin said. "I remember the first time I drove here after I had returned."

Peter said nothing, looking out of the window.

"It's the colour," Colin said. "One forgets how green it can be. I'll bet you never saw anything like that in Europe."

"No. It was different."

"It's the light."

He was still upset by his impetuous coupling with Phyllis, still flattered by her response. Again he saw her little finger sticking out away from the knife she held, heard her lapses of grammar, the rising, Frenchcadenced ends of her sentences, the "*ouis*" and "*nons*". For the first time he wondered about his unwillingness for Phyllis, his attraction for Anna, the glamour of her background, her degree in Law, her parents' wealth and social position, her acquired taste and elegance. He was not sure how much Anna had been cause of, or later reinforcement for, his attitude towards Phyllis. He was sure only that, having met Anna, he had not wished to let her go.

"All this land you looking at gone, you know."

"Oh yes?"

"Foreigners. They've bought all the damn place."

They had crossed the mountainous central hump of the island. They were descending to the Atlantic coast. He told Colin of the incident in the metropolis in which neighbours had got together to purchase a house which an immigrant couple from the islands wished to buy.

"Well they can buy all they want here. Nobody prevents them. Once they have the money. Sometimes only by pretending to have it."

He snorted.

"It's a bloody joke, man. We're not serious here."

Peter could catch glimpses now of the sea.

"I managed to get a few small pieces," Colin grinned.

Peter recognized the grin. He asked,

"Small?"

"Well," Colin prolonged the word, "you know. If you want any, you'd better hurry."

"I'm broke."

His glimpses of the rude Atlantic were more frequent. They were on the coast. They passed through small villages consisting of huts on either side of the main road. The big car, unwieldy in the hills, sped over the flat, coastal road and, passing through the villages, was as obvious, and as prestigious, as a priest's cassock.

The rough Atlantic, almost continually glimpsed now, soothed a little his remembered uneasiness. It might have been by the sudden precipitous lift of rock at one end of the small beach they had just passed that a Colonial Governor of slave times had sat, alone, on his horse, in the desolate and early morning majesty he described in his diary, lamenting his loneliness and yearning to look again at the Channel coast of England. Duty, so he had written, compelled him to stay on the island, a bachelor, pacing the verandah of Government House night after night, unable to sleep, alone, forced, for administrative reasons, to keep himself aloof both from his compatriots whom he commanded and with whom he had more than a skin in common and from the creole landowners and businessmen with whom, he had written, a skin was all he shared. And he had died, that dutiful and principled man, worn out by disease and by his efforts to preserve justice on the island, ironically, within the sphere of a greater injustice he had nowhere in his diary questioned.

The road turned inwards again and began to climb once more. The sea disappeared altogether. In a short while and after many turnings they were high up and Peter could see it again far below, white against the out-thrusts and running up narrow strips of brown sand between them.

"We'll breakfast at Keith's," Colin said. "Keith Austin, remember him?"

"Of course. Must be quite old now."

"About sixty. But as fit as a fiddle. He has nothing to bother him."

The road had become much narrower and very difficult. Perhaps, Peter thought, watching Colin turn the steering wheel furiously and hearing the frequent sounding of the big car's horn, perhaps it had been along this old road that, the day before his solitary musing on the small beach, the dead Governor had passed with his escort, in full ceremonial attire. The slaves lined the road to wave and sing at him. They loved him, he had written, because he was fair. Peter imagined the white tunic, trousers thin in the leg, the red band over one shoulder, the sword, the decorations on the chest, the white, plumed, helmet. And he saw the spurs as the Governor held his horse in check before the shouts of the noisy slaves.

It was not thus he liked to look at the dead man. Peter, too, had yearned, living in the metropolis in which his fear, not any duty, had kept him, for the oasis of relaxation and friendliness the island, from a distance and in a time that was of memory only, seemed to offer.

"Here we are," Colin said.

The car came to a stop in the centre of a short, pitched semicircular road in front of the door of the hotel. A maid in white cap and apron appeared.

"Morning, Mr Colin."

"Hello, Doris. Where's madam?"

"She was here just now."

"She's busy?"

"No, sir."

"Tell her I've brought somebody to meet her and Mister."

They sat on high stools before a curved, polished counter. Doris was about to leave.

"Won't you serve us first?"

Doris giggled.

"The usual, sir?"

"Brandy and ginger, Peter?"

"I thought you said breakfast."

"That will follow."

"O.K."

"Yes, Doris, the usual. Make them doubles."

"Yes, sir."

Mrs Austin came in.

"Here's madam."

Peter and Colin got down from their stools.

"Hello, Colin."

"Morning, Gloria. This is Peter."

"Peter Breville?" Mrs Austin smiled. She had not lost her island's accent even after more than twenty years on this one.

"Welcome back, Peter."

As they shook hands, Peter felt they had always known each other. It was so easy to be accepted in the still small group of returned professionals and their wives on the small island. He understood the use of first names between Colin and Gloria.

"Thank you, Mrs Austin."

"Gloria." Her face became more lined as she smiled.

"Keith's listening to music. All he ever does now. Which leaves me all the work."

She was still very handsome.

"Work?" Colin was incredulous.

"Yes, Colin," she smiled, "work. Let's sit down. No, not at the bar. Here. Doris, bring the gentlemen's drinks."

Her small figure generated authority, efficiency. She was still vigorous.

They sat on easy chairs around a table covered with an embroidered tablecloth. A vase of flowers stood on its centre.

"Doris, you haven't changed the flowers."

"Yes, mam."

"Did you?"

"Yes, mam."

"Anyhow, get some fresh ones. These look a little stale."

Doris removed the vase.

"The drinks are on me," Gloria smiled. "Yes, Colin," it seemed she anticipated in a routine well known to herself and Colin, "there'll be a repeat as well. You'll have to have breakfast alone though. On me too. And you'll come back for lunch. It's only a twenty minute drive back from."

"Nearer an hour," Colin said.

"Let's say forty minutes." She pronounced it forteh, like the people from her island. "I'll tell Keith."

"Nice old woman," Peter said, when they were in the car again.

He had seen Gloria from close up once only, standing with a group of other women outside of the church. They all had handbags hanging from their forearms and they all wore gloves. He had not remembered what the occasion had been that had brought the wives of the more eminent members of the island to congregate outside of the church in the middle of the morning. But Gloria's (it was Mrs Austin's then) light-skinned elegance, increased by the fame, in the small town, of her husband, had remained with him.

"Nice rich woman, too," Colin answered. "All this land belongs to them. It stretches for miles and it goes in deeply on both sides of the road. I'll show you where it ends."

They had drinks before lunch sitting at the end of the back verandah other than that where the table had been laid. They looked at the flower garden and, beyond it, at the first of the banana fields. The little man with the square shoulders and white curly hair asked questions about the metropolis to which he had not been for several years.

"We were last there in 19—."

The well-articulated words contrasted with the light sing-song of his wife, gift to her of that other island she had abandoned to make her life here with this very successful man who was several shades darker than she was. Keith sat back in his chair, spare and hardy-looking, his pipe, which he said he must stop smoking so close to dinner, on the table next to the chair.

As a boy Peter had heard much of Keith Austin. There had been non-white lawyers before him. But he was the first black one and, though they spoke about the wife he had chosen, the people were proud of him. Austin had become a member of the legislative council, an office he had held until the island had been granted universal adult suffrage. Earlier he had been one of the first non-white men to become members of the town's Social Club. When, at nearly forty, he went to England to read for the English Bar, he had already stopped practising.

"It was a matter of principle," he said. "I never even used the English qualification."

He had been articled as a clerk after leaving secondary school and had taken some local examinations. He would not have been allowed to practise anywhere else if he had not done the English Bar.

"But you know, boy, it was always the land. I was born here, spent all my holidays here on the small piece of land the family had. I came back and I bought. It was cheap then and I gave good prices. Nothing, mind you, like what I should expect now..."

His wife fretted about lunch waiting on the table to be served.

"I guess I was always a peasant at heart. Let's have another punch."

The friends, doctors and lawyers, who passed, were always in a hurry. They had another drink. He had made the rum punch himself.

"I brought back two things from England of any value," he said. "The Bar Exam. was a formality. I didn't need it. I did not ever use it. I brought back Gloria and some records. I developed a taste for music in Europe."

He had met Gloria in Europe where she was holidaying with her father, a senior Civil Servant. Gloria was no longer young. Keith persuaded her to marry him.

They went to lunch. They ate boiled yam, beef, stewed with carrots and turnips, and salads of lettuce and cucumber. There were no courses. The dishes were all on the table and you served yourself. They drank soursop juice mixed with sweetened condensed milk and with bits of ice floating on its surface. After lunch they went back to the other end and drank a French digestif while they looked at the garden.

Colin drove back to court in ——. Gloria, too, got up and went inside. Peter and Keith talked bananas for a while. Then they walked past the garden and into the first of the banana fields. Peter pointed, talked, asked questions, answered others, reassured, congratulated Keith. He gave Keith a list of books he might like to read.

They went back to the verandah. They talked briefly about politics on the island. Keith thought it was a mess. He was disdainful of the "carpenters and clerks who ran the country now". He regretted the granting of adult suffrage.

"We were not ready. We still aren't."

And he spoke with nostalgia, though without any apparent bitterness, of the days when "at least you had well-educated and capable men in Government."

"You have only opportunists now, boy," he said. "I'm glad I'm out of it. I couldn't become a hustler. Not me."

He got up.

"Would you like to listen to some music?"

Peter was unwilling to refuse.

"The records are not in very good condition. They're quite old in fact."

It was strange to sit in Keith's study, the windows closed, and listen to Bach's Brandenburg concertos in the semi-dark, while he sipped a large brandy and ginger. He had sat and listened to that very one next to Anna in the small metropolitan church, ignorant of, and bored by the music, observing the rapt faces of those who listened. He could smell the tobacco smoke from Keith's pipe. He closed his eyes. Nothing that had happened to Keith on the island, so far as the story he had related earlier was concerned, had prepared him for the music he so obviously enjoyed.

The music sounded. Peter listened and sipped his brandy. The scent of pipe smoke was pleasant. He tried to imagine Keith and Gloria in the metropolis the first time they met there. It was not only with mulatto wives that professionals returned now. It was with white ones, too, as well as with black. Keith had married late. Perhaps, Peter thought, remembering the story Duncan had told him, he might not have contemplated marrying a black wife and had not dared to get a white one.

From being overtly and aggressively resentful, Duncan, after some pints of beer, had begun to relate anecdotes, some of which made Peter laugh, of the father he, apparently, must once have loved.

"Give your people a chance," he quoted old Desmangues as saying to his mother, speaking of Keith's attempts to get into the Social Club, "and they forget the rest of you. They think only of themselves. What the hell he wants to join the club for?"

At that time, Duncan said, old Desmangues had already ceased to go to the club. It seemed he was already isolated, caught between the disapproval of his clubmates and a latent antipathy for the people of whom one was the mother of his children. He was, besides, much older than most of the members of the club who disapproved of his unhidden liaison with Duncan's mother, of his frequent visits to, sojourns even in, the house he had purchased for his illegitimate family. He had long replaced the comforts the club had provided him by the pleasure he derived from his children in the house or on the estate.

"They don't have half of Austin's brains anyhow, most of them."

He considered most of them upstarts (he was very much older than some of them), rough, uncultured. He had not been schooled in Barbados or Trinidad. He had had all of his schooling in England, had completed his studies at Oxford from which he had come down as a lawyer. He had never practised. And it was only after his English wife and their two children had left him and returned to England that his liaison with Duncan's mother had begun.

Peter listened to the music. Old Desmangues had dared to cross the line, driven by whatever loneliness his wife's departure may have left him with, to Duncan's mother. He might not have foreseen the implications fully nor the contradictions of having children he loved with a woman the colour of whose skin he disliked. He might not even have intended that there should have been children. Or perhaps he had seen all the possibilities and was too old, or too wealthy, to care. He had gone over to Duncan's mother and had lived for years with her in the big house in the town as though she were his wife. His colleagues' disapproval had not stopped him. But Keith, his membership to the Social Club assured, still had not dared to cross the line. He had had to be content, keeping to his side, to get as close as he could, through his mulatto wife, to it. But Colin had returned with Helen. And Peter would have married, if he had been able to, Anna. He wondered whose wife she was, or would be.

The music flowed. He recognized this third concerto as another of those he had listened to with Anna in the metropolis. He sipped his drink. It was nearly finished.

The pipe smoke was pleasant. The sound of the recorders evoked again the blond female soloists standing with the rest of the orchestra in front of the altar and, too, costumed masqueraders, covered in dried banana leaves up to their necks and dancing on sticks their friends held while a woman played for them. The woman was blowing on a bamboo flute, not elegantly, like the German soloists, nor with their practised composure, but furiously, her black face intent under her colourful turban, her eyes closed, and her head moving up and down and from side to side in the sunlight.

The music stopped. He heard the old man shuffling to open the window. Through it, his own eyes open now, Peter had a glimpse of green on green against blue and, framed briefly by the window, like the returning bats he used to see sometimes, on mornings, of floating, tobacco-blue, pipe smoke swirling towards the open. Gloria was waiting with tea downstairs and with cakes that she had just made. While Peter sipped the tea that brought the perspiration to his skin, and nibbled the still warm cakes, she prattled on, in her island's accent, amiably. Peter watched her. Her husband smoked. She prattled pleasantly. He listened.

And not much later Colin arrived to drive him back to the island's capital.

10

Colin came to collect Peter and Phyllis just before seven on the evening of the next day. Paul was working late again. His mother, looking a little worried, had told Peter so while she was clearing the table where his father had just eaten. Peter had been about to ask what had happened, if anything had, and then had changed his mind. Perhaps his father, whose car he had seen pulling out from the kerb as he approached the block of flats, had commented on the food. He had gone upstairs instead. Now, dressed, he sat on the verandah waiting for Phyllis to come down and for Colin to come for them. Michael was telling him how much trouble the small turtle gave him that he kept in an earthenware pot in one corner of the verandah. Michael had to change the sea water in the pot every other day. He fed the turtle raw fish, sometimes bits of bread. On some afternoons he went to one of the two canals that joined the sea to catch tiny fish for it. Did Peter know how he used to catch them? No? He used to watch them swimming together, a stone in his hand, then he would throw the stone just outside the group they formed, swimming, and hoped that one or two would be thrown up with the splash on to the other bank of the canal. You had to be careful how you threw the stone, he explained, because it was not kill you wanted to kill the fish, but throw them on the other bank.

So you had to try to throw the stone under them as they were swimming. Peter thought it was easy, eh? It wasn't easy at all. Michael was sure he couldn't do it. He was telling Peter how he used to watch the big turtle, it was big because the fish was so small, eat the tiny fish when Phyllis joined them.

"Eh, eh, Aunty Phyllis, you looking nice, eh."

"Why you didn't go to Rosary and Benediction?"

"It too late now."

"Why you didn't go before? With your granny?"

"I was talking with Uncle."

"You were talking to Uncle? Your uncle only just came down. He was with me upstairs."

Michael lowered his head, half-smiling, looking censured.

"You think you smart!" His aunt told him.

Michael had been right. Phyllis looked very well indeed. Peter told her so. He had made love to her again, the night before, after his drive with Colin from Keith Austin's, because she was next to him on the bed and it had seemed absurd for him not to. He had made love deliberately, preparing her. And afterwards she had talked to him, talked until his eyes closed and he did not hear her and awoke again and heard her quiet voice and knew he had dozed. She told him of the children and of her illness. She apologized for their deaths as though she were responsible. She spoke of his mother; about Paul and his father. Her own mother, she explained, had left the big house, about to fall down, and gone to live with a policeman on the other side of the river at the back of the town. Her brother, Lucas, was in the States. She did not know any more about him. She asked about Duncan. Peter said he had met him now and then in the metropolis. He did not elaborate. He wanted to sleep. She told him her mother was pregnant again. She came sometimes to the store where Phyllis was working. Peter fell asleep and did not get up until the next morning when he made love again to Phyllis before she went to Mass.

Colin arrived. They drove to his house. Sydney was there, a glass in his hand, talking to Helen on the verandah and removing, every now and then, with a characteristic gesture of the left hand that Peter well remembered, the hair from over his eyes. Helen smiled and waved. They climbed on to the verandah.

"Hello, Helen."

"Nice to see you again, Peter."

"My wife, Phyllis."

"Hello."

"*Pine Boeuf*," Sydney said, laughing and shaking Peter's hand. Peter and Colin joined Sydney in a burst of laughter. Since Peter had come back it was the first time that anyone had called him by his nickname, in the island's patois, his schoolmates, who said his penis was like that of a bull's, had given him. Helen, who alone did not understand, was laughing, seeing the others laugh. Phyllis was smiling uncertainly. She disappeared with Helen through one of the doors. They had all entered the drawing room.

"What happening?" Peter asked Sydney in the island's patois.

"Ask Colin, boy, not me," Sydney answered in English.

"Me? Why me?"

The conversation was going to be in English from now on. Sydney was not really familiar with the patois of the island. He only knew a few words and phrases. The three friends were laughing.

"Because it's you boys in charge now, that's why."

Sydney slapped Peter on the back, "So how's the old *Pine*, man?"

"O.K. How's the family business?"

"Can't complain too much, you know."

"Not when you're shipping bananas by the tons every week," Colin said.

Sydney laughed, about to sip his drink. Peter and Colin were serving themselves.

"Listen to him," Sydney said to Peter. He winked. The girls came back.

"What're you girls drinking?" Colin asked.

"Sorry the wife couldn't come, man, Peter, for you to meet her," Sydney said.

"Who was so blind, Sydney?"

"She's from Barbados," Sydney laughed. "You don't know her. She's not feeling too well."

His sentences sang and lifted almost like Phyllis'. It was merely a more correct version, the educated islander's, uncorrupted by sojourns of any length in Europe or North America. It was what Peter's and Colin's speech would have otherwise been. But, already, Colin was showing much less of the metropolis in his language.

They laughed and drank a great deal at dinner. It was the companionship of their schooldays. They did not venture beyond the easy superficiality of jest, the comfort of reminiscence. They did not have any business either to discuss. And so, in the recesses of a stopped time his remembered nickname had helped to evoke and where, now, they had met again, the shared joke, the remembered prank, like the gesture of Sydney's left hand to his hair, was familiar, reassuring, established again the surface togetherness of the classrooms and the playgrounds. They covered difference, perhaps even antagonism, with their bantering tone.

"Remember that football match against...?"

They tried to recapture the excitement of the first two draws and of the marching and drumming in the streets after the narrow victory that had given the school the championship and the trophy for the first time.

"Who scored that goal again?"

"It was..."

"Yes. But it was Paul who made it."

There was no pause in the conversation. There was nothing, looking at the past, that, if you wished, you could not not see. They talked about the partnership that Sydney had formed with Paul, the best batsman in the school, when they played cricket on the concrete playground with tennis balls.

"You boys could never get us out."

"Us?"

"We used to get you out often enough. It was only Paul who was giving trouble."

"He was good..."

"And you were smart."

"...better than all of you. He had class."

"I'm sure they don't play bat-for-ball now," Colin said. "Every little boy in the street has a tennis ball now. Perhaps," he smiled, "you wouldn't get a batting now, Sydney. It wouldn't be you alone who had tennis balls."

And they talked about the days during the war when you couldn't get any tennis balls to buy.

"They used to play tennis with balls without any fur on them."

"I know why Sydney had balls all the time," Colin said. "His father kept them specially for him. He knew Sydney couldn't get a batting otherwise."

They laughed.

"I used to bowl you out," Sydney said.

"Stone us out, you mean."

"You used to think each batsman was a mango you were pelting stones at."

"Used to get you out all the same."

"Only Paul..."

"Who was Paul, Colin?" Helen asked.

The pause was only slight.

"My elder brother."

"I didn't know you had a brother, Peter."

"Nor even a wife, Helen, I'm sure."

"Nor even a wife, you secretive man." She smiled. She knew about Anna.

"Remember Ernest?" Colin asked.

"He used to spit on his cakes in order not to give a piece to anyone else."

"No!"

"Yes." It was Phyllis. "The girls used to talk about him in the convent."

"Now how did the convent girls get to hear a thing like that?"

"We used to hear a lot of things."

She had been speaking in low tones for most of the time to Helen. More than once, observing her, Peter had remembered Clive, walking next to him along the wet, cold February street of the metropolis, his ageless head bobbing up and down above the upturned collar of his coat, saying, "I want a woman I won't be ashamed of. A woman I can take out, man. I'm not snobbish. You need things like that."

"What happened to him again?"

"Who? Ernest?"

"Yes."

"Wasn't he expelled?"

"I mean after that."

"I don't know."

"Oh, he's around," Colin said. "If we'd been lucky we might have seen him yesterday, Peter. He works in the country. I see him sometimes on the roads. I think he's a road overseer or something like that with the Public Works. Things don't look too good."

"It's amazing how those things affect you later on," Colin said. "At the time it's not nearly so important."

"No."

"The place is too small."

"Unless you belong to the right family."

"Or are rich enough."

"Yes."

"If it were Sydney who had stolen another boy's wallet and been expelled, he could always go away, to another island or even to Europe. Ernest had no place to go to."

"I have to agree," Sydney said.

Peter laughed. "I've just remembered..." he said.

And they talked again about their schooldays. Apart from their religion and the fact that they had been born on the island, it was the only common ground between their separate and different existences. And after dinner, over drinks on the verandah, they trod it some more. It was the first time that Peter was talking to Sydney outside of the school premises and away from the playing fields; the first time he had seen Sydney at night apart from Speech Days or, sometimes, in the church. He had waved to him sometimes on the main street of the town outside of the family store. And on Sundays while he and Colin played with other boys on the sand, he had seen Sydney playing with his friends and those of his parents before the only hut on the beach. Occasionally, running along the sea's edge from one end of the beach to the other and back again, and passing in front of the small white community before the beach hut, he had waved to Sydney.

They sat on the verandah until, at nearly eleven, Sydney rose to leave. Peter and Colin walked down to the lawn with him.

"Come to the office before you leave, man, Peter. I'll show you around. You can have a chat with the old man. Perhaps we can go across to the Blue Nile for a drink."

He got into the car.

"Thanks again, man, Colin. Sorry about the wife. I'll tell her how much she missed."

The car moved off. As Peter walked back over the lawn with Colin, Colin said, "Those boys know how to adjust."

"How do you get on?"

Colin raised his hands away from his sides and dropped them again.

"You get to know the boys, man. You learn to be smart like them."

The pattern had not yet changed. It was still "you boys" on both sides. Even though the beach hut and the Social Club had disappeared, the groups were still separate. They were like opposing teams running, from the starting point of owners and owned, in lanes on a track where the curve was only an optical illusion and the staggering was an advantage to some and a disadvantage to the others. Even now the distance between them, between Colin and himself on the one hand and Sydney on the other, still remained. Even though Colin, too, now, retired to his home in the suburban hills as Sydney had already been doing after school on afternoons long before.

"Well, Peter," Helen said when they climbed again to the verandah. During the dinner, her accent had marked her out whenever she spoke. She alone had shown no trace of the island in her speech. And, to anyone listening to them from another room, she would have stood out alone, different and apart, and the only stranger.

"How very, very nice to see you again!"

Once at one of the many discussions they held in her and Colin's bedsitter, she had said, "But you're really so much like us in so many ways. Sometimes if I close my eyes, Colin might be just another Englishman."

She and Colin had not long been married. She had come with him to the metropolis where he was doing postgraduate work. She disliked the capital, wished to return to the provincial town where she was born and in whose University she and Colin had studied. She was sitting next to her husband on one of the two single divans which, they had explained, at night they joined together to form a bed. Colin had just come in with Peter. He wore a dark suit. Both himself and Peter, with gloves on and seen only from the shoulders down, might conceivably have been metropolitans. Even when they spoke.

But Colin had objected.

"I'm no black European."

And Anna, when she heard of Helen's remark, had said, "She must say that. After all, she's married to Colin now. She must justify that. Perhaps she'd like to make him one."

Yet, to Peter thinking about it, it had seemed that Helen was not wrong. That a process of copying and imitation, begun on the island's sugar plantations, continued still. The barely understandable language of the first slave cunning enough (dressed in his master's discarded coat and using sounds and gestures he had imperfectly imitated) to interpret his master's orders to the rest of the assembled slaves, had been replaced by the islands' dialects and, for a few islanders, by language acquired over years of study in Europe and, in some cases and absurdly, over months alone. These were the new interpreters, direct descendants of that first expediently opportunistic slave, admired and feared, like him, by those to whom they interpreted, and, not infrequently, a source of amusement to those for whom they did.

And no one knew for how long they would continue to be the clowning interpreters most of them were.

Their discussion that day in Colin's bedsitter had been longer than usual.

"What you want," Helen said, "is a past."

"But we have a past. There's Africa."

"And Asia and Europe…" She smiled. "And you have others as well."

"Well," Colin had prolonged the word.

"Well?"

"I suppose you're right."

"Of course I'm right. You have, collectively, nothing to break away from, nor anything to hold on to. Take the Jews…"

And it was then that Colin had said, making a joke, "Perhaps we are our own past."

"You are," Helen had been serious. "Your past, as a people, shall have only begun with you, now."

Peter smiled as he loosened his tie and took the drink that Colin had brought to him on the verandah. They had had conversations like the one he remembered often. Anna had been to only one of them, however.

"It's a waste of time," she had told Peter.

"How does it feel to be a West Indian?" Peter asked Helen.

And the four of them sat in the pleasant shadow on the

verandah and talked for a long time. It was after one when Colin drove Peter and Phyllis back to their home in the town. He and Phyllis made love again and Peter kissed her for the first time.

11

He remembered Daphne and Anna the next day only when, from the small motor launch that was taking him to his parents' village, he looked at the uneven line of the coast it went past. Daphne had often wished she could visit the island. He imagined himself and her in a canoe, similar to the ones he saw now, close to the cliffs and hearing the water explode in holes in their sides.

Anna in an open boat, here or anywhere else, he could not imagine. A certain carefulness, an instinct for avoiding unpleasant or uncomfortable situations had always qualified her. Anna was never adventurous. And Peter would not have known with her the world of sexual improvisation he had discovered with Daphne.

And yet, during that first uncomfortable walk, the leaves swirling over the lawns and making noises beneath their feet, Daphne's unprepossessing body had promised nothing, her quiet smile given no intimation. The wind blew, the gulls, which had reappeared, swooped, wings outspread; or they landed, nervously aggressive, among the staider water fowl. A woman was throwing crumbs to them. The red face of a man struggling to row his family against the wind made Daphne and himself laugh.

He had not known then that she, too, was an alien in the metropolis; had had to wait for a long time before she talked of the house she had lived in on the west coast with her parents. Long before then, he had heard her repeated determination to sue for maintenance the father who was married to the stepmother she had fled from. Only gradually had Daphne's hurt dependence emerged from behind the oft-repeated, empty threat.

His togetherness with Daphne, unlike the passionate interlude he had known with Anna, had been one of companionship, built around the silence in the bed-sitter they shared as he caught up with work Anna had interfered with; on the sudden disruption of a comment that made him raise his head; in the nightly association under the blankets of his and Daphne's bodies. One evening, returning later than usual to their bedsitter, he had barely entered before she threw her plump body against his, the displeasure, like the fear, in her voice and eyes.

"Why didn't you phone or something. I couldn't think what had happened. I phoned the hospital..."

And her dependence, unhidden, had demanded a concern which Peter had never felt for Anna. It had always seemed to him that Anna would survive and survive glitteringly. And he had only feared he might lose the brilliance she provided him with.

It was Daphne who, holding his hand as if it belonged to her, laughing and enjoying his discomfiture, pointed and made comments as they walked through areas of the metropolis where immigrants from the islands lived.

"Look at those houses! Just look at them!"

"Spade."

She used to call him that often after she had surprised him with it for the first time.

"Spade."

"Be careful, Daphne."

"Do you object?"

"No."

"You're my spade."

The cause of all spades had seemed to be hers. She would come into their bedsitter, sucking her teeth, and tell her latest story of intolerance and prejudice.

"Be careful. You don't want to antagonize."

"I don't care if I antagonize. It's a shame."

Anna preferred to walk elsewhere in the city.

"It depresses me," she said of any immigrant area. "It's always filthy, always ugly." And,

"It's no use pretending. I didn't come here for that. I didn't come here to stay. I can do nothing for them."

Instead she dragged him to the concert hall, the playhouse, the art galleries. Her mother had taught her how to play the piano.

"I studied this music," Anna used to say, "I was brought up on it."

Neither his ignorance nor his insensitivity had diminished the pleasure standing and sitting next to her had given him. She had been like the sun of a wet, metropolitan summer. Hers was the instantaneous, the glance over the shoulder of her admirers, the little pinch as she passed in the crowded room, the short note after weeks of silence; and the intense weekend in his bedsitter after months of absence, itself broken, characteristically, into intense bits, never prolonged, like splinters of many-coloured glass he sharpened a never dwindling desire and pleasure on. He could imagine her contempt if she had known of his relationship with Daphne.

"I loathe them," she used to say, speaking of metropolitans, of the men especially, dwelling on the verb until it seemed to vibrate, prolonged in her vocal chords by the hatred that had summoned it.

"She's so wonderful!" She was disdainfully imitative, repeating the comments about herself she had overheard. Then she added in her normal voice,

"They're all so damned patronizing!"

What irked, she told him, was an admiration not meant for her to hear but expressed just loudly enough for her not not to overhear. It was not even the admiration of a repressed desire. It was the admiration for a freak.

"As if I had three legs! They disgust me."

Her hatred for the metropolitans was total, the courtesy and the indifference that masked it, complete. She wished to continue to amaze them, make them always confess their admiration which, in turn, would enable her to loathe them more. He had been glad that his place, unlike that of the immigrants she avoided, was close to hers. No boyhood dream had contained himself neglecting his postgraduate studies in a metropolis to be with a girl like Anna.

One Sunday morning he had watched her sitting before the mirror in her flat combing her hair. She was annoyed. An African student with whom she had quarrelled had called her the daughter of slaves. She sucked her teeth.

"They, too, feel superior. Their condescension is even worse. 'You have no country. No ground is sacred for you. Your old people come here to die.'" She was imitating the English of the educated West African. She was fuming.

Peter left the bed and went to stand behind her and cup her breasts in his hands. She let him. The reflection of his arms, cut off by the mirror's upper edge, just above Anna's reflected head, seemed of hands that did not belong to him. It seemed he was watching someone else play with the breasts of which his own hands felt the touch.

"I damn well know what I am," she said.
"Daughter of slaves!"
"Exactly."
Peter looked at the strange hands over the breasts he held, at his truncated body reflected behind Anna's seated figure. It could never be important to him what part of the world she had come from. And then, his hands, at the first hint of her impatience with his embrace, already moving away from her, he heard her say,
"I won't allow myself to be used by them or by anybody."
Except me.
The thought surprised him. His squeal of triumph was in his mind alone. He put one hand again on her breast, looking at the reflection in the mirror. In the mirror, she, too, looked at it. Then, placing the other hand on her other breast, he bent to kiss her shoulders, his eyes closed, full of a sense of unreality, of playacting that yet was not playacting. The always unbelievable event of themselves together, both naked, in a room become their world, his world, was heightened by the fact that it was the first time he had awakened in her flat. He opened his eyes. The unusual reflection – of his hands over her breasts, his head over her shoulder as she continued, sullen still, to pass the comb through her hair, the fuzz between her slightly-opened, indifferent legs – all that he saw in the mirror seemed to complement Anna's back which, in the flesh, he felt against him. All else, beyond this moment of his possession, was inconsequential. She might be African, what did it matter, or Chinese, or English… His eyes closed again, his kisses on her bare back multiplied. He was murmuring to himself between touches of his lips on her black skin.

"What are you murmuring about?" she asked him.

Caught in a sudden access of wind, the motor launch moved from side to side. Peter looked up from the water. The launch had moved farther away from the line of the coast. The sea foamed on rocks at the foot of cliffs. A statue of Christ, and a cross, stood on one of them. The passengers crossed themselves. The boat turned, following the line of the coast. But the rocks disappeared, the boat came close to the shore once more, the sea was almost placid again. The women were talking in patois and laughing again. A man was telling them funny stories. Peter recognized him. He had been a young porter when Peter still played on the wharf in the island's capital.

"Antoine," he called.

The women stopped talking to look at him. Peter had been taking no part in their conversation. Antoine looked questioningly, his dirty undershirt hanging over oil-stained dungarees. Then,

"Not Peetah?"

Peter smiled and confirmed nothing.

"Is Peetah. Is Peetah self."

They shook hands.

"Eh, eh. When you come?"

Peter told him. The women looked at them. Peter had tried to speak patois. But, for too long, he hadn't spoken it. His mistakes marked him out. And when he spoke English his accent was no longer completely that of the island. He was a stranger.

"So you going to see your father and mother family?"

"Yes. But I've never been there before."

"True?"

"Yes."

"You don't have to worry. I'll show you."

"Breville's child, *oui*," Antoine turned to the women. They knew his people. No friend, Peter was no longer a stranger. Soon he was laughing openly at Antoine's jokes.

He was standing on the small wooden pier of the village waiting for Antoine to finish working when he heard his name.

"Dr Breville?"

He turned. The black priest was smiling. Peter's answering smile covered his surprise.

"I read in the papers that you had come."

"Oh yes?"

They moved to the edge of the pier out of the path of a push cart laden with bags of flour.

"You don't remember me?"

"I'm afraid not."

Peter's smile was discreet, the language he spoke, more correctly formal. His English made hardly any concessions to the island's cadence or its pronunciation. He might have been a boy again coming home from school and lapsing into patois to speak to his mother.

"D'etaing. Thomas D'etaing."

The name was not familiar.

"I was in form three when you left school."

They shook hands.

"Did you see a priest on board?"

"No. But I travelled second class."

"He must not have come. Staying with us?"

"Only for a day and a half."

"Only?"

"Yes."

The small crowd on the pier was thinning now.

"Are you waiting for somebody?"

"My guide. I've never been here before."

"Your parents are from here. I know that. We talk about you a lot here."

Peter smiled.

"Maybe I can help you. I was born here."

"Thanks. But I had already arranged..."

"Of course. You remember Fr Mouret?"

"Yes. Is he here?"

"Yes. He's in charge here. He'd like to see you."

For a long time Fr Mouret had conducted classes in religious knowledge in the secondary schools of the island's capital.

"Why don't you pay us a visit at the presbytery to morrow?"

"I'll see if I can."

"Come. We may be able to go for a drive into the country. If Fr Chauve comes by car between now and then. He's the priest I came here to meet. You see, I'm learning to drive."

"I think I should like that," Peter said.

"I'm sure Fr Mouret would like very much to see you again."

He walked away, answering greetings from all sides. Soon, with Antoine, Peter was walking up one of the streets that climbed away from the beach.

At nearly eleven o'clock, the next morning, he went to the presbytery. Fr Thomas was with another priest, a young Frenchman, standing in the yard next to a battered car. Peter and Fr Chauve shook hands.

"We were just about to leave. We thought you weren't coming."

"Fr Thomas was telling me about you."

The language of the young Frenchman impressed Peter. He did not always remember the language of the priests on the island, all of them Frenchmen before he had left it, to be as good as Fr Chauve's.

"Have you been here long?"

"We came together."

He cuffed his black colleague on the shoulder and smiled.

"We've been here almost for a year," Fr Thomas said.

The relaxed togetherness of the priests was strange to Peter. Always, so far as he could remember, their cassocks had marked them apart on the island and an austere public image had kept them there, at a distance, reached only by the respect, fear and admiration of the majority of their congregation. They had been remote at the altar, in the pulpit, the confessional. And they had been remote on the streets, marked out by their cassocks and by the colour of their skin.

"Will you come with us?"

"Yes."

"Good. We'll see Fr Mouret when we come back. It's late already." Fr Thomas laughed. "He can wait."

They got into the car. They soon left the small town and were following the uphill road, climbing steeply, turning frequently, to enter a lush foliage, smelling of damp and almost spilling on to the narrow, rutted road.

"Your bells awakened me this morning," Peter complained. The priests smiled. Peter, sitting in the back seat saw the Frenchman's grin reflected in the driving mirror.

"We had some Requiem Masses."

"The bells just tolled and tolled. They sounded as though they were in the next room to mine."

"I know. They do make a lot of noise. But the people like it."

"Do they?"

"Yes."

"You'd be surprised how much they do."

"How do you know?"

"Well, there are various kinds of Requiem Masses. There's one without any bells at all. But nobody ever asks for that one."

"I can understand that. It's not the same as not disliking the bells. Perhaps if you abolished the hierarchy of the bells... After all a mass without bells makes a social comment, doesn't it? You pay more for the bells, I believe."

"They'd still want the bells," Fr Thomas said. "A requiem mass without bells is not the same. They've told me so themselves. I try to tell them it doesn't matter. They don't listen. They want their bells."

"Perhaps you could give it to them some other time when I'm in the village," Peter laughed, "at one o'clock, say, or two."

He had watched groups of men and women, dressed in mourning, on their way to mass. Their shod feet, the ties and socks of the men, the frocks and hats of the women, contrasted with the barefooted seller of fishcakes and bread, the street sweeper, hatless and with her tattered dress and her long broom, the ragged, barefooted fisherman hurrying, his bamboo mast over his shoulder, down the slope of the otherwise empty street.

The car stopped. They had turned into an unpaved path ending in a clearing almost at the edge of a hill. Protected by the foliage behind them they smoked, leaning against the car and looking across the sea at the blue indistinctness of the neighbouring island. They looked for a while, surrounded by the smell of damp and of rotten and rotting vegetation, commenting on the beauty of the view.

"It's a favourite spot of ours," Fr Thomas said.

The priests took Peter to a point where the hill dropped on the landward side. Over the tops of the foliage he saw the small town in the valley below them.

"There's the presbytery."

They saw it enclosed within its stone walls in the centre of the small town.

"And the school."

"Where?"

"There."

Next to the presbytery and the church, the square, with its fountain, was a small patch of green. Trees showed here and there among the houses.

"And the hospital."

It was at the edge of the town.

"There seem to be a lot of people."

"Yes. Today is clinic day. The doctor came this morning from the capital. It was with him that Fr Chauve came."

"It looks as if it will rain," Fr Chauve said.

"We used to have a resident doctor here. But he went back to the States."

It was dark before much longer and, over the sea, it was grey in the distance. The indistinctness that was the other island had disappeared. They went back to the car.

"You'd better drive, Fr Chauve."

"No. You drive. It's good practice for you."

The rain, sudden and heavy, caught them less than halfway down the hill. Water ran freely down the windscreen and the rolled-up windows. They were perspiring inside the car.

"You better take over."

The priests exchanged places. Then the car went down the hill slowly. Peter could see nothing through the windows. They could hear the rain on the roof of the car. When they reached the town ten minutes later, the rain had ceased already to fall. They lowered the windows again. The wind on their faces was cool. Fr Chauve sneezed.

"You're catching a cold."

"Yes," Fr Chauve sneezed again as he was saying it.

Naked children were still running on the streets. The water was muddy in the swiftly moving canals. Branches and bits of vegetation floated on its surface. It was bright again. Steam arose from the wet asphalt.

"The Anglican Church."

It was a small building, of stone, at the end of a street on the very edge of the town. Behind and around it the wet vegetation gleamed in the sunlight. They entered the presbytery yard.

"Perhaps you'd like a drink?"

"Certainly."

"First, shall we say hello to Fr Mouret?"

Fr Mouret was not in his office.

"Well. You'll see him before you go then."

The two priests shared a room at the back of the building. From it, beyond the back verandah, they looked on vegetable and flower gardens which stretched almost from the edge of the building to the mossy stone wall. Above the wall, the green hills glistened in the post-rain sun. They each had a small glass of French rum and when Peter rose and left the room, only Fr Thomas followed him out of it. Fr Chauve shook his hand and allowed the two islanders to go out together. They passed again through the office. But Fr Mouret still had not returned.

Outside, the streets and pavements were dry again as if it had not just rained torrentially. The trickle of water in the canals on the sides of the street was still brown. The two men walked past the almost indecipherable din of the sing-song voices of children repeating after their teachers.

"I used to teach here once."

"Oh yes?"

"Long ago."

"You sound as if it were ages."

"It feels like that sometimes."

He laughed.

"I'd just left school. I was fourteen. I was a teacher. I was important, very important."

"Yes. I think I can remember teachers were a very important thing once. Not many of us could hope to go beyond being a teacher."

"No. I shouldn't like to be told now what I used to teach the children though."

It was a primary school they had passed. The children were reciting a nursery rhyme. Their voices were becoming less and less loud.

> *"... and Jeel, went op a heel,*
> *To fetch a pail of wahtah,*
> *Jack fell long and broke his crong..."*

"I never even imagined then that I should one day have been a priest."

"Didn't you choose to be one?"

"Yes and no."

Peter smiled.

"I know," Fr Thomas said. "But that's the true answer. A series of accidents."

"Accidents? Design surely."

They laughed.

"Design if you like," Fr Thomas said. "But it was still wonderfully strange."

"Tell me."

"Well, in the first place, long after I had given up any hopes of being able to get to secondary school, I went. As an Intending Teacher. You must remember the Education Department's Intending Teachers Scheme?"

"Yes. You went to secondary school for three years, then you went back to teach. But I seem to remember a lot of boys stayed on for more than three years, did School Certificate, sometimes even the Higher School Certificate, and did not return to teach."

"Actually," Fr Thomas said, "I was one of those who stayed on to do School Cert. But I came back afterwards to teach."

"Here?"

"Believe it or not."

"Oh, I believe you." Peter laughed. "I shouldn't dare."

"I was twenty. I came back to be assistant headmaster in the middle school here. Then one day Fr Mouret called me and asked me about becoming a priest. Even now I cannot remember having shown any particular vocation. But I wasn't the only one he spoke to. It seemed the Church was beginning a new policy. Some American sects had come and were sending local recruits back to America to be trained. Those sects were growing."

"I remember the time. The priests warned us from the pulpit, talked about excommunication."

"I believe it was worse after you left. I took another year to decide. Then I decided it must be better to go to France and become a priest over several years than to remain as a teacher here. I went away."

"And you've come back."

"Yes. And have discovered how much easier it was for me to take the decision to become a priest than to return as one to this island."

"How so?"

"I suppose I could be dishonest, pretend that the church must mean for me the same thing that it means for my French colleagues, the older ones especially. And yet..."

"And yet?"

"Let us say that it is more complicated for me to be a priest here than it can be for them. That doctor I mentioned just now, the Church made him leave. He was a Seventh Day Adventist. The rumour began that he was trying to convert the patients he attended. In the end he and his wife, a nurse, had to leave the island. And now we have no doctor in the village. That's fine for the church. Fr Mouret has won a victory for it. What do you think it can mean to me? Just another victory for the Church?"

"I don't know?"

Fr Thomas smiled.

"Perhaps, for you, too, I'm suspect?"

"For whom are you?"

"Some people here who thought I could have prevented the doctor from having to leave."

"No. You're not suspect for me. I only know that the Church demands loyalty that is absolute. It does not allow loyalty to it to be shared with anything or any body else. One can only serve or leave her."

The priest laughed.

"It's almost as if you're giving me a lecture."

Peter smiled.

"You know I didn't mean to."

"It was a joke."

Then he added, "I can't leave, of course."

"I don't suppose you can."

"Merely by wearing this cassock I'm doing some thing. The people here saw me bathe naked on the beach. A lot of them bathed with me. Their attitudes to priests can never be the same again."

They had come to the entrance to a yard. The priest stopped.

"I did do what I could about the doctor. I talked to Fr Mouret. But I have also taken the vow of obedience. You'd never know how much in a trap I felt."

He took Peter's arm.

"My home's inside here," he indicated the yard, "would you like to see my mother?"

The yard ended in a circle, like a balloon blown up at the end of a long neck, fenced by houses. A little girl arose from where she was stooping in front of one of them and ran to hold the priest's hand.

"Say good afternoon."

"Good afternoon, sir."

"My niece, my brother's child. He's working in a factory in England. Her mother has gone to meet him. After they're married and have settled they hope to send for her."

They entered the house.

"Where's Mama?"

"I'm here, oui," his mother's voice came from the other room speaking patois. She appeared pulling a dress down about her. "The rain wet me so much when I went to buy fish." Then she saw Peter.

"Eh, eh. I didn't know you had somebody with you."

"You remember Mr Breville's son I was telling you about, Mama?"

"It's he?"

"Yes."

They shook hands.

"Your mother and father and I were good friends," she told Peter in patois. "They well?"

"Yes, thank you."

"So you is a doctor?"

Peter explained that he could not cure people. He was not a real doctor.

"So why they calling you doctor?"

He and her son laughed. But he could not explain to her. The language they were using did not allow him to.

"We were taking a walk and I took him for you to see."

"I just come from the beach to see if I could get some fish." She laughed, "Is rain I get instead. I brought back a little thing to warm me and your father when he come back." She looked around her. "Where's Stella?"

Her granddaughter appeared in the doorway. Fr Thomas laughed and put a hand in his cassock.

"Go and buy mangoes," he told his niece. They heard her run out.

"All right, Mam," Fr Thomas said.

"Is only a little white rum to warm your father when he come back. But I must offer the gentleman something."

She produced two small glasses and a beer bottle corked with paper and containing white rum.

"You ever used to hear priests used to drink, sir?"

They drank.

"Give me your glass quick, you hear, before Miss Inquisitive come back."

She went outside with the glasses and returned drying them with a piece of cloth. The beer bottle had disappeared.

"We must go, Ma."

"Already, Father? Wait *'on*, your father must be coming back just now."

"I've already stayed too long."

"So is only fire you and your friend come for, Father?"

The two men stood up. She followed them into the yard.

"When you coming again, Father?"

"I don't know, Ma."

Peter and the woman shook hands.

"Goodbye."

"*Au revoir, m' sieu.*"

"I'll tell my parents."

"Yes."

The two men walked out to the street.

"She won't call me anything else," Fr Thomas said, "not even when we're alone. Nor will my father."

"Old habits..."

"Sometimes I feel they think they must set an example for other people, to ensure I don't get less respect than the other priests."

They were walking uphill again, in the direction of the presbytery.

"Sometimes, though, I wonder."

"What about?"

"I feel sometimes I have abandoned them."

"Your mother was very proud."

"My father too. And they both feel I've honoured them."

"In that case."

"But I'm uncomfortable sometimes. I feel, at those times, that a priest is not something my parents can afford. I feel like a luxury, an extravagance. Do you understand that?"

"Yes, I understand that."

"And it's a luxury I offered them, not one they chose to have."

"It's obvious that they like having it, though."

"Yes, I know.

"But you're still troubled?"

"Yes. How shall I put it? I feel I'm an end instead of a beginning. And yet, at the same time, it is very obvious to me that I am a beginning, not an end. Does that make sense?"

"Not a great deal."

"Being a priest seems somehow abortive. I should have been a bridge, like you, a link between our parents and the children you alone will have."

Peter said nothing.

"Now you alone, of the two of us, are that bridge. I am like one side only of a bridge. I project from one bank and I end over the chasm. But you can go to the other side. You will join what you have known to that which you will never know. I dare say I'll end up like Fr Mouret. Perhaps I should have remained a teacher."

"You really believe that?"

"I suppose not. I should have faced no contradictions, though, if I had. I should have had to serve no divided loyalties."

They were outside of the presbytery.

"Perhaps," Peter laughed, "you're just a bad priest."

"Perhaps. Or a bad something else."

"What?"

The priest laughed.

"So you're leaving tomorrow?"

"Yes."

"And then?"

"In three days' time I leave to take up an appointment in ——," he mentioned the island to the north where he had been an undergraduate.

"Even so."

"Yes," Peter laughed. "Even so."

"And you won't come back, not to work?"

"No. Not now anyhow."

"So be it. I won't be able to see you off tomorrow. So, goodbye."

"Goodbye."

"God bless you."

"Good luck."

12

At home, in the capital once more, his mother told him about Paul. Paul had begun again to put on his suit to go to work. She was crying. Peter did not understand. She explained. Paul had gone to work that morning as usual, in his shirt sleeves and his khaki trousers. He had returned at about eleven, put on his suit, a tie, and had gone back to his work in the dirty warehouse. He would be going to work like that, fully dressed, for about a week. She had not wished to tell Peter anything. She had hoped he would have had time to leave the island before "the thing took Paul again".

Peter listened. It became obvious that Paul should have lost his job in the warehouse many times over and that it was Sydney, it could only have been Sydney, who kept him in it. Peter glimpsed, too, the completeness of his father's indifference; the conspiracy between Phyllis and his mother to keep the truth, as they had been keeping it from Michael, away from him. Paul's confidence was absolute, resided in himself alone, depended on no conformity to conventions, nor on any success at secretly transgressing them. Peter had no doubt that his brother was mad. And he was appreciative because behind the easy joviality of his remembered nickname, Sydney had been very discreet. Peter went to thank him.

Sydney waved away his thanks, laughing. They were

standing in the main office just outside the door that led to Sydney's smaller one. Typewriters clicked about them on several desks.

"I couldn't do otherwise," Sydney laughed. "And it's not charity either. He works when he's all right."

He patted Peter's arm.

"Don't worry, Peter. Come on, let's have that drink I promised you."

They went to the *Blue Nile* across the street. Half an hour later Sydney crossed the street again to his office and Peter walked back to the house. He walked along the hot streets past men and women in bare feet and indifferently dressed. He overheard their patois expressions. The street was lined on both sides with parked cars. There were large American and English refrigerators, in the windows of stores he went past, standing next to gas stoves. From posters, American men and women gnawed smilingly at American chicken. A sign in one of the stores stated that you were stupid to buy a TV. set when you could rent one.

He might have been walking in a hot, drab, imperfectly imitated miniature of a metropolitan shopping centre.

"They think I'm mad," Paul told him that evening on the verandah, still in his tie and his suit. "All right. I encourage them to think so. I behave as if I am. Deliberately."

His voice contained neither the musical lilt of the island nor the mispronunciations that the French had bequeathed to its English speech.

"This is the only world I can inhabit now, where they can only laugh and tolerate. I can never fail or disappoint now. Nobody expects anything of me. Not even myself."

"You know that's a lie."

"Of course it is. But it's only I who know that."

They were speaking in low tones. From the room behind them they could hear nothing of what Phyllis, Michael or their mother did. The windows, like the door, were closed.

"It's useful," Paul said. "It saves others as well. Your mother cannot regret my failure now. Only explain it. She cannot blame; only feel sorry. I enlarge her world, grant her possibilities of existence she should not otherwise have had. She can't be indifferent now. I heighten her awareness, her sensibility." He laughed, "You see, I'm like a God. And at the same time I escape her contempt and that of everybody else. I can never be a disgrace now, to her or to anyone else. Except your father. It is only for him that, dead to myself and to others, I am very much alive. When I put on a suit and go and sit in that dirty warehouse and people stare and snigger, it's he that's tainted. It's his image, that neat, creased image of his achievement, that's sullied. Not I. If I could, I'd will myself to live a hundred years. And him to live as long."

His voice was low and steady.

"And Michael?" Peter asked.

"Michael will have to survive as best he can. We all do."

"And that's all your answer?"

"Yes. What do you think? *You* may have other answers now. Not I. I have opted out. Of everything. I don't care now. I cannot care. I dare not care. Not even for Michael. If I begin to care again, about anything..."

He shook his head. His voice had not risen. But Peter, now, was undeceived.

"No, I can do nothing else. Otherwise I'd go mad for true."

It was Paul's first concession to the island's idiom. As if his confrontation with what would face him on the island if he relaxed his impersonation was already reducing his world of unreality to fit it within the island's triangular confines.

"It's the only way I can live with your success and with that of all those others who have returned from abroad to parade it. And it is the only way I can stomach and, at the same time, affect your father's."

It was like being cornered by Paul, when they were boys, in their parents' absence.

"I hate him."

Peter was quiet.

"I don't know whether you can understand what it is to be suddenly and completely alone," Paul said. Then he laughed.

"I'm not alone any more. I only seem to be. The laughter of the town is a bond which joins us. But there was a time when I was alone, when I almost went mad from being alone. Your father might have helped. But he didn't care. Perhaps you haven't forgotten our quarrels at the time."

"No, I haven't."

"He didn't care. He would have thrown me out. And I couldn't stand your mother pleading with him on my behalf. And so, I was alone. I went to church in desperation. Your mother was relieved. Your father might not even have noticed. And the town watched. They understood the language of sin and punishment. My meekness and my humility pleased them. But I observed them observing me walking every morning to church and Holy Communion, my missal in my hand. I began to cater to their interest. Laughing secretly, I postured for them to see. You must remember some of my antics. I refused to look upon your mother's anguish, revelled in your father's growing embarrassment. After you left I exaggerated my performance. And I laughed secretly at him. Finally I accepted the job in the warehouse. I begged Sydney for it. It was my decision. He believed it was his. Nobody knew that it was I, not they, who dictated now.

"It was easy. I discovered the absence of responsibility. I pretended I did not exist. It was better to be nothing than to be what I knew I could only become thinking always of what I might have been. I became nothing. I am nothing."

"And what does that make Michael?" Peter asked after a while.

"I said he'd survive. I have to survive first."

"And that's all your answer!"

Paul's voice was raised for the first time.

"Yes. I know. You accuse me tacitly of selfishness, leave unasked questions about responsibility. I know what you infer. But people in glass houses... What about Phyllis?"

"What has she got to do with you and Michael?"

"You think you're too good for her, too educated. You've left her alone here for eight years!"

Peter stood up.

"Sorry," Paul said. "It was an opportunity to hit and I seized it. You must know how much I envy you."

Peter sat down again.

"And yet," Paul said, "I was so sure once, so confident... There was nothing for me to envy."

He had been confident enough to refuse to marry Patricia, Michael's mother, whom he had made pregnant. It was then that Patricia's mother, herself unmarried, had reported him. She took Patricia with her to the

Headmaster of the secondary school where Paul had been teaching for only seven months. Paul was offered a choice of marriage and keeping his job or having to resign. He refused still to marry Patricia. He was dismissed. The town talked about it. The normal thing would have been for Paul to have married Patricia as Peter, later, had married Phyllis.

Paul had misjudged his confidence, however. His nonconformity made him an outcast in the small town. Peter had watched the arrogant confidence of his brother disappear with each unfavourable reply Paul had received to his letters of application. For a long time, as his efforts in the yard where he practised had been, Paul's collapse had been secret and personal. Peter had watched him spend long hours alone sitting in the door of his room and staring out at the yard as if upon the perpetually departing back of the person he had been. Then the drinking and night clubs started. It was like an explosion. Paul might have been in a metropolis where no one knew him. And, at home, the quarrels with his father multiplied. Peter used to sit quietly and listen. His mother no longer even tried to interfere. And then, suddenly, the nightclubbing, the drinking, the violent quarrels in the house, had ceased. For months Paul went every morning to church and Holy Communion. It had been as if a page, literally, had been turned.

The rest of the story Peter had heard in letters from his mother. One day, Patricia, who had developed the habit of coming, sometimes, when Paul was out of it, to the house, left Michael there with Peter's mother and then had walked to a corner of the wharf, unobserved, to throw herself into the water.

"May I take Michael with me?" Peter asked his brother.

"Yes, if you like."

★

That night Peter made love again to Phyllis and he heard her, rocking beneath him, say between moans, "Peter, I love you. I love you, Peter."

He was embarrassed, put a hand over her mouth. And, their lovemaking over, he moved away to be cool again. The room trembled on the beat of the Power Station that came through the window. And then she asked,

"When are you going?"

"The day after tomorrow. You and I. And Michael." There was a pause. Then she said,

"Perhaps this time will be better."

"Perhaps."

"I may even be pregnant."

And the fear, Peter thought, the fear, and the memory, and the suspicion. It frightened him exceedingly that she might be pregnant. As if this pregnancy, as yet only possibility, travelled hummingly along lines to join the fear and the panic of the first. It was like listening, in the dark, to a record one had made long ago. The sounds he listened to evoked gestures and postures he did not wish to remember. Lying on his back on the bed, he felt suddenly weary. He was about to say something to Phyllis when there was a noise from Paul's bedroom and the light in it went on.

He wondered how much Paul had been listening to them.

ABOUT THE AUTHOR

Garth St Omer was born in Castries, St Lucia in 1931. During the earlier 1950s St. Omer was part of a group of artists in St Lucia including Roderick and Derek Walcott and the artist Dunstan St Omer. In 1956 Garth St Omer studied French and Spanish at UWI in Jamaica. During the 1960s he travelled widely, including years spent teaching in Ghana. His first publication, the novella, *Syrop*, appeared in 1964, followed by *A Room on the Hill* (1968), *Shades of Grey* (1968), *Nor Any Country* (1969) and *J—, Black Bam and the Masqueraders* in 1972. In the 1970s he moved to the USA, where he completed a doctoral thesis at Princeton University in 1975. Until his retirement as Emeritus Professor, he taught at the University of Santa Barbara in California.

ALSO BY GARTH ST OMER

A Room on the Hill
ISBN: 9781845230937; pp. 162; pub. 2012; price: £8.99

A Room on the Hill is a devastating portrayal of an island society (much resembling St Lucia in the mid 1950s) suffocating in its smallness, its colonial hierarchies of race and class and firmly in the grip of a then reactionary Catholic church – which insisted, for instance, on different school uniforms for the children of the married and unmarried, and three grades of funeral. The novel focuses on a small circle of the educated middle class, whose response to colonial society ranges from acquiescence, finding cynical self-advantage in the new anti-colonial politics, suicidal despair and various shades of rebellion. Its astringent realism in questioning the direction of West Indian nationhood is finely balanced by metaphors of as yet untapped potential.

At the heart of the novel are two characters, John Lestrade, who feels trapped between his desire to lead an authentic life and his despair that this may be impossible on his island, and Anne-Marie D'aubain, who unremarked by the other characters, shows the possibility of a courageous existential revolt against the absurdity of circumstance.

First published in 1968, St Omer's novel is distinguished by its sensitivity to issues of gender, its elegant concision and, in its existential questioning, an intensive focus on the inner person. If the world it describes has gone, *A Room on the Hill* lives as a major attempt to bring modernity to the aesthetics of the Caribbean novel.

Shades of Grey
ISBN: 9781845230920; pp. 194; pub. 2013; price: £8.99

As Stephenson comes closer to his girl-friend Thea, with her easy talk of three generations in her family, he has to acknowledge that his past is a blank. He has never known his father, not lived with his mother, and cannot remember what his grandparents looked like. He knows, too, that his failure to come clean about a disreputable episode in his life threatens their relationship. *The Lights on the Hill*, the first of two interdependent short novels in *Shades of Grey*, is a moving and inward portrait of a man, blown along by circumstance, trying in his halting way to construct his own story.

Another Place, Another Time goes back to the character of Derek Charles, who appears as a returning islander in St Omer's first novel *A Room on the Hill*. Here, almost a decade earlier, St Omer explores the circumstances in which the scholarship boy makes the decision to separate himself from his family and friends and conclude that "He had no cause nor any country now other than himself." As in all St Omer's fiction, there is a sharp focus on the inequalities of gender, and a compassionate but unwavering judgement of the failings of his male characters.